*Pride Publishing books by Cheryl Dragon*

**Single Books**
One Weekend
Runaway Cowgirl

**How to Catch a Cowboy**
The Long Ride

**Anthologies**
Out of Bounds: Making the Pass
Hard Evidence: Under His Protection

# How to Catch a Cowboy

# THE LONG RIDE

CHERYL DRAGON

The Long Ride
ISBN # 978-1-83943-920-9

Interior text design by Claire Siemaszkiewicz
Pride Publishing



Published in 2020 by Pride Publishing, United Kingdom.



Pride Publishing is an imprint of Totally Entwined Group Limited.

# THE LONG RIDE

# Chapter One

Sitting on the rails waiting for his ride, Lucas Burr watched the opening fun. He owned a quarter of the rodeo that had put Burrwood, Texas, on the map…at least the rodeo map. The stands needed to be full and the crowd happy—not for his ego, but for the rodeo.

His mom rode into the grand opening, leading the little kids' rodeo group for parents to cheer. Burrwood Rodeo was known for being overly safe with the kids' events. They took place earlier in the day and with more safety than required.

The announcer whipped up the crowd into gushing over the kids and how they ranked in their events. Lucas couldn't help but grin. That had been him once, only he'd traveled around Texas with his dad competing against guys older than himself. The prize money had helped keep the family ranch going. He liked being around smart and daring men and the adrenaline was a rush every time.

"If that isn't the finest set of rodeo kids in Texas, just ask Miss Betsy and she'll tell you. Thanks, Betsy Burr and the rodeo kids of Burrwood!" the announcer shouted.

Betsy waved to the crowd. The other rodeo riders cheered too. Burrwood Rodeo was also known for its family atmosphere, even with plenty of young bachelor riders. Lucas hated policing the ones who got drunk early or were a bit too handsy. Some men didn't have any respect anymore, but this was Texas and, thirty or sixty, Lucas wouldn't stand for it. But after what Lucas had done to one drunk cowboy who disrespected his mother, the other cowboys minded their manners.

"Ready?" the old goat asked.

Lucas turned and nodded to his manager, Greg Simon, who looked very much like an old goat. Long white beard, always chewing tobacco, and wiry and nimble.

"Another day, another ride." Lucas shrugged it off. "Attendance is up. Kids' group is bigger than ever. We're newer than most but we're attracting more riders and bigger crowds."

"I told you, safety. People like a scary fall now and then—a little drama just like a crash at NASCAR—but most of the falls are harmless, just like a spin-out at the races. When it comes to the kids, they like their children's program extensive but extra safe and run by rodeo moms." Greg nodded.

"You were right from the start there." Lucas liked his mom running something and she loved the cheering crowd and attention. He hadn't worried too much about it at the beginning, because of course they kept the kids super-safe. But last year one creepy employee out at an East Texas rodeo had been found dead after being accused of touching a rodeo kid.

The guy hadn't made it to jail—he hadn't made it out of the rodeo once the parents had heard about it. People thought horses and bulls could kick—pissed-off parents were the most dangerous thing. Taking matters into their own hands might shock some people but not true Texans.

"Keep an eye on Mom and who she lets volunteer." Lucas looked at Greg. Mama listened better to Greg when it came to business chats.

"Sure enough, but it's only the moms and she's got plenty willing." Greg chuckled.

"Safe? I want us to be the Texas standard," Lucas insisted.

Greg sighed. "Adults make their own choices and earn a bigger purse for bigger risk, but we run safe. Having paramedics and an ambulance always on site makes it so much easier for sponsors to buy in. Lowers the insurance. We look like pros, not hicks." Greg spat chew on the ground. He was crowing over his suggestions.

Lucas shook his head. "Only in Texas are you a professional."

Greg gently punched Lucas' shoulder. "I've known you since you were ten. Your daddy taught you to ride and rope. I taught him how to make the most money at it. Respect your elders."

Grinning, Lucas nodded. "I do, and I know I pay you enough to trim your beard and get a haircut. Any new ideas for the rodeo?"

"I'm getting trendy. Growing my hair out for a manbun next," Greg joked.

A few guys looked over and snickered.

"I believe you're joking, but the fact that you know what that is worries me," Lucas replied.

"Rodeo is hot. Cowboys are a trend. Leather, rope and tight jeans. Ladies love ya. Men want to be you. We need to get videos up more. Not just fan stuff, but tape our events professionally and get interviews. Sell pictures of you guys," Greg said.

"Banged up and bruised? Smelling like horse sweat or manure? Sure," another guy commented.

Lucas wasn't discounting the idea, but it was more for outsiders than the fans who paid to get in. "Video ain't got smell to it. We can talk about it later," he said to Greg.

The announcer boomed over everyone else. "First ride of the night is Tim Hayes. Tim is a Burrwood native who works as a firefighter when he's not riding. Let's see how long he can stay on his bull."

The buzzer blared and the gates opened. Tim and Lucas had grown up together in the rodeo circuit, always competing and always friends.

"You got it, Tim," Lucas called.

"You're up next. Be safe." Greg moved away.

They loaded the bull, snorting and stomping, into the chute. Lucas mentally prepped himself. The zone was his old friend. Just him and the bull, no crowd or anyone else. Certainly no thoughts about his mama watching. He'd been hurt so many times over the years that he knew it was mind over matter.

Broken bones would heal, bruises went away and drinking a few beers was better than getting hooked on painkillers. He refused to think about his dad except to know he was up there, looking out for him. Lucas blocked out that one wrong kick to the chest. His dad had ridden too long and his reaction time hadn't been what it was, according to Mama. The helpers in the ring hadn't been fast enough to distract the bull that day either. That was what Lucas remembered then blocked out.

That day would haunt him until he died, and he knew it.

The crowd cheered and Lucas looked up. Tim fell off and hopped back to his feet, letting the staff distract the bull while Tim flashed the crowd a big smile as he made it to safety.

"Nice ride," Lucas said.

Tim nodded and clapped Lucas on the back. "Good luck."

Everything was right, boots to hat, as Lucas climbed on. He closed his eyes. This wasn't a fight. It was a challenge to join that animal for a short time, to feel the world through its power and raw nature. The bull snorted and kicked out its back legs hard, then its rear right leg on the rails.

"Easy, you'll get to toss me soon," Lucas teased.

The buzzer went off and Lucas relaxed his body but gripped the rope on the bull as the shoot opened. It was a fluid state that got his body jacked around like a nasty car crash. Greg's analogy was right. The key to less injury was not to tense up.

The bull jerked right, over and over. Lucas adjusted his body and anticipated the move. Then it changed to a full kicking and bucking front to back, normally a horse move.

Lucas shifted and held on, but the bull shifted too and shook side to side while stomping. The complicated pattern made Lucas tense up for a second and that was all it took. He felt himself lose his seat so he let go of the rope, or he'd be dragged and trampled.

The helpers ran out while Lucas tried to tuck and roll, but the rump caught him. Better that than a hoof, but it threw him off his calculated fall and laid him flat out on his back with a hell of a lot of pain.

His hat flew away as his head hit the dirt.

* * * *

Jack Gable liked his routines, from the early morning runs to Monday-night grocery stock-up and Wednesday mix-it-up night with a couple of friends at Rainbow Rose, the only bar in Burrwood that dared to do things that weren't heteronormative.

Being gay, out and single in a tiny Texas town wasn't easy, and Jack's mother repeatedly tried to talk him into moving back to Dallas. As he parked his old pickup outside the physical therapy office attached to the Burrwood long-term care home, Jack wondered what kept him here. He'd come when his uncle had been hurt and refused to comply with PT. He'd moved here, got a job and worked with his uncle until he was back at work. Life moved a tad slower here and Jack stayed as though something here was meant for him…but he was getting lonely.

Walking through the staff door, he waved. "Morning, all."

"Find any hot dates?" Teddy teased.

"No luck." Jack rolled his eyes. Teddy was a nickname because the new PT guy looked like a big teddy bear. He was also very chatty.

Brenda looked at the schedule. "Nursing home patients again, with Kevin. I'm being punished for something."

"The permanent patients need to work their muscles as well," Teddy argued.

"Want to trade?" Brenda grabbed some coffee.

Teddy looked at Jack for help.

"We all do our turn with the residents. This town isn't really big enough for an outpatient PT. The hospital has some staff and we take care of the rest. Teddy's working with the replacement crew, knees and hips. That's pretty dull stuff but he still needs my supervision." Jack warmed up his travel mug of coffee and headed to flip on the lights in the outpatient room.

Teddy joined Jack in the room with his bear claw pastry and coffee. "They do get the residents more than we do."

Jack nodded. "She's easier on them, so they probably request her. Some people can't be tough *and* nice. Kevin is quiet, but if a patient tells him no, he walks away like a mouse. Bren pushes a bit but then they call her a nag. It's mostly little old ladies so Bren does better there, chatting with them about hair and men. She can motivate them if she tries but we can't ever force a patient."

"But you like to play it tough," Teddy joked.

"I am tough. You're positive and friendly, plus, a former football player. The athletes will respond to you. That's a different challenge than octogenarians who don't want to move because of arthritis pain. Once you're going on your own, you'll get guys who want to be back at it now. Don't worry. Just remember to pump the brakes when a patient's pushing too far. Too much too fast can do more damage," Jack reminded him.

He tilted his head with his trademark smile down to a thin line—he hated conflict. Brushing the crumbs from his beard, Teddy seemed lost in thought. He didn't like to scold motivated patients or take sides.

"Time to open. Just focus on your patients' needs and you'll be fine." Jack clapped Teddy on the shoulder.

At lunch, Brenda complained about her assignment again. Teddy rolled his eyes behind her back. After Jack finished up his turkey sandwich and chips, he refilled his water bottle.

Just then the boss, Ken Webb, poked his head in. "Jack, I need you for a meeting right after lunch. We rescheduled your two next clients."

Jack arched an eyebrow but held back on how he really felt. "You did? Why?"

"We'll talk at the meeting. Don't worry about it," Ken said.

Jack checked the clock. "I'm ready now if you are."

Ken frowned. "Don't want to infringe on your lunch hour. You have ten minutes left."

*Might as well get it over with.* "If it's important enough to reschedule two clients, it's worth ten minutes."

Jack followed him to his office. Ken wasn't a bad guy, and far from the worst boss he'd ever had. Despite being retirement age with solid white hair and a gray handlebar mustache, Ken didn't call every woman *sweetie* or *doll*. He didn't think because Jack was gay that he couldn't do the job, which involved touching patients. Some men got squirrelly about it, but Jack was the best. Ken was in charge of the physical therapy portion only so the nursing home managers didn't interfere with their work. But Ken liked to remind people at times that he was the boss and mix up the schedules to prove it. Luckily, Ken cared about the patients enough that he generally chose in their best interest.

Jack sat in the guest chair. "What's up?"

"We have a new client coming in who is higher profile in Burrwood. He's a professional in the rodeo and wants to get back riding. He's very eager, rather cocky, and needs someone firm but fair. He's used to pushing his body, being injured and getting right back on the bull, so you need to meet him where he is. Get him on board," Ken said.

"Do you have his file?" Jack wasn't going to react to warnings or conjecture. The reality of the injury, orders and prognosis were the facts.

"Let's wait on that for a moment. You might recognize the name. He fell, had a concussion and was paralyzed from the waist down for a few days. The swelling came down and he regained full movement but the pain and the damage to his spine is real. His manager is worried about getting him up riding again and the doctors have told him another fall could paralyze him forever. Some discs are bulging and it's all a matter of where the impact is."

"Rodeo idiots," Jack muttered.

"That right there won't help. Your straight talk might help him see the reality but he's not someone you can just toss back to the doctor. You definitely can't bully him. His docs will bend over backwards to help him get back to work. This rodeo stuff is his living," Ken warned.

"Then he'll be used to pain and working through it," Jack said.

"Most people would agree with you, but some pain meds get a hold of people so fast. I'm just warning you that this guy isn't our average patient. He's someone we really don't want pissed off," Ken said.

There was a knock on the door. The secretary, Lexi, poked her head in. "The manager is here and wants to speak to you first."

Ken nodded.

A wiry guy with a bolo tie, boots and a long white beard walked in. "Ken, thanks for the help."

"Sure thing, Greg." The men shook hands.

Jack stood up and shook Greg's hand.

"Greg, this is Jack Gable. He's the absolute best. Jack, Greg manages the best riders in the Burrwood Rodeo," Ken introduced.

"A pleasure." Jack sat back down.

Greg sat next to him. "Good choice. Lots of muscle. Is that a military tattoo?"

"Army right out of high school. That's where I started my medical training." Jack flexed out of habit. The rainbow flag next to it usually got more attention.

"Good. Lucas can be tough, but you're tougher." Greg nodded.

"I'm immune to cowboy charm. I've lived in Texas all my life, army deployment excepted. Tough, I can handle," he promised.

"He wants to get back in the saddle yesterday. Riding bulls at the rodeo. You understand that's dangerous without an injury?" Greg asked.

Jack smiled. "I understand. I've volunteered to sit with the paramedics if they're shorthanded at the rodeo. I'm a qualified EMT but I prefer the PT office. If he wants to risk his neck again, once his body is healed, that's on him. My job is to get him there. He must limit activity and cooperate with the levels of treatment he needs to regain his strength. Sometimes that back needs to rest. Being even temporarily paralyzed and stuck in bed for one day takes the body days of intense PT to recover from."

"Rodeo boys think they're made of rubber and steel. Getting him here was a miracle. I have to take his mama to church for a month for this." Greg shook his head.

"That won't kill you. If she works to motivate him, give me her number." Jack shrugged.

"I like him. He's a pistol but all business with eyes on the goal. Lucas will try to bully, negotiate, impress and charm. Don't fall for it. He's a handful," Greg warned.

"It's all business. He can fight me all day—it won't help." Jack smiled.

"Our toughest and our most professional. If anyone can wrangle him, Jack's the one," Ken said.

"And if for some reason it's not a good fit, I'll recommend who I think could work well with him. I'm about what's best for the patient," Jack added.

"Why don't we bring him in and the two can chat?" Ken suggested.

"Sure, he should be here by now. Insisted on driving himself," Greg replied.

Jack looked at Ken. "I'd like to see his chart and orders before I meet him."

"You're approved but the hospital chart system seems to be slow adding you. He's not prohibited from driving," Ken said.

"Nah, but his back hurts like a dog's leg caught in a bear trap. Every time he moves." Greg nodded to the door. "I'll go see."

"Is he taking his pain meds as prescribed?" Jack asked.

"He doesn't like fancy pills. Tough guys just pop open a beer and power through with a few aspirin." Greg headed for the door.

The door closed and Jack turned back to Ken. "A rodeo guy who's self-medicating with beer? No."

"Yes, this is a huge get for us. If we get the rodeo guys to come here and get treatment, it's a lot of new clients," Ken said.

"Can't we get ones who follow the rules and take the right thing for pain?" Jack pressed.

Ken held up his hand. "Give him a try. Meet him. See if he's fixable, charm him and push him to do it the right way. He's Lucas Burr—Burrwood is named after his family. He owns a quarter of the damn rodeo that doubled the size of this town."

Jack sighed. "I grew up in Dallas. Burrwood isn't that impressive."

"Do *not* say that. If Lucas comes to us, every cowboy who aches will come to us. To you. Huge bump in business. Most of those guys blow off PT. This would only up your value here. You want to move up?" Ken dangled the career carrot. People had speculated about when he'd retire himself...maybe this was a step in making those plans—getting someone in on the business to pass it off to?

"Of course, but if he doesn't take his meds, we're going to have a problem. We can try Teddy. If he wants someone who falls for the charm crap—maybe Bren? Just don't think I'm your only option," Jack said.

Lucas Burr was the hottest rodeo rider in town, also one of the most sought-after bachelors. Tough, rugged and good-looking without being a pretty boy—Jack had heard plenty about him from his friends, patients and the local news. This was a potential problem. The coverage of his recovery and if he could ride again wasn't just about Lucas—people would be watching. Considering the amount of pre-meeting meetings, Ken and Greg were worried. That told Jack a whole lot.

Ken chuckled. "Don't try to push every tough case away or boot it back to the doctor. You can handle him. He wants to ride again—he's motivated."

"Motivated often really meant expecting a pain-free miracle. Men hate feeling weak." Jack shook his head.

"You understand that, which is why we don't want Brenda to get her claws into him. Men love being cared for by women. Lucas is known for being a ladies' man," Ken explained.

"Sure but Teddy could help." Jack nodded. "We'll see what sort of man this Lucas Burr is."

He decided right then to treat him as though he were a total stranger, which he was, but as if he wasn't the least bit famous. Jack couldn't be impressed or the power sway would be wrong. That might check Lucas' ego long enough to give Jack the upper hand. Then again, if Jack acted all impressed and star struck, Lucas might open up and let Jack in a bit more. Jack was flexible with his approach to patients but he needed a plan for the hot cowboy he'd googled on his phone during this long prep session.

# Chapter Two

Greg opened the door and Lucas walked in behind him. He tried to minimize the limp and keep the cane behind his leg. Medical visit or not, his instinct was always to appear strong. Real men didn't let weaknesses show—Lucas tried to turn off his dad's influence but that little voice in his head was always there.

"Lucas Burr, Jack Gable and this is Ken Webb, the manager," Greg said.

Jack shook Lucas' hand and Lucas gave his usual firm handshake, even though he wanted to pull away. Jack's skin was soft but his hand was strong—the spark had to be static electricity. The guy was in incredible shape, of course, but when they locked eyes, it felt different. Lucas held the eye contact with confidence, but it only made the spark grow. His entire life he'd been coached to take the lead and dominate in every situation, and this would be no exception.

"You've never roped or ridden in your life," he said with a grin.

"I've never even been to the rodeo except to help out as a paramedic. I think we met once. You needed stitches on your leg and refused the ER until after the rodeo. But the rodeo isn't part of my job requirement. I'm fully trained to help you get back on the horse or bull. We'll get you better. Trust me." Jack winked.

Men winked at ladies of any age and little kids—not at other men. Lucas cleared his throat and took in the muscled man in scrubs who had winked. Jack's arms showed off tatts, the rainbow one hard to mistake. Looking elsewhere, Lucas knew the guy was hot. Jack being gay made Lucas uneasy. "I have a brother in the military. Thank you for your service."

"You don't have to say that. I mean, I appreciate it but I'm lucky. I had a good experience and skills, and now I have a job I love. Like you love the rodeo," Jack said.

Looking into Jack's eyes showed Lucas it wasn't bragging. That matter-of-fact tone was honest. His deep green eyes were so clear and pure—no secrets or stress. Lucas envied him. Jack seemed at peace and Lucas always felt the internal struggle to live up to what his father wanted and fight his urges.

Jack triggered those urges and Lucas tried to ignore it all, but he took in the details. Jack had a few faint freckles on his pale skin that contrasted with his dark reddish-brown hair. It set off the green scrubs well. He never looked at men that intently. Not really.

He turned his attention to Ken.

"I'm sure Jack is great, but I asked for a woman," Lucas said.

Ken cleared his throat. "Mr. Burr, I'm Ken Webb, huge fan. Truly, I would only give you the absolute best. In your case, we don't have a woman who could catch you or support you if you pushed yourself too far in an exercise. You're a tall and very muscled athlete. Jack is tough and smart but he's also very strong if you need to lean on him. This sort of pairing reduces the chances of injury while you're recovering. He'll get you where you want to be as quickly as possible."

"As quickly as is safe and possible," Jack corrected.

Lucas cocked his head at Jack. "You're bossy."

Jack smirked. "I'm sorry, I don't follow the rodeo. I've helped professional athletes before so I can handle whatever you have wrong with you and manage your expectations," he said.

Lucas folded his arms and leaned to one side. Catching himself, he glanced at Jack. He'd seen everything from the limp to the cane. The tough guy would nag and hound him as well as any woman.

"How exactly are you going to handle me?" he teased.

"I'll review your chart, develop a PT plan and, as long as you follow it and do the program, we'll get you back to work as soon as possible," Jack replied.

"I need to be back on the circuit in a week," Lucas said. The sooner this temptation was away from him, the better. Lucas knew that doctors weren't supposed to mess around with their patients—that probably extended to physical therapists too, but Lucas didn't want to find out. He'd play it safe and be done before he lost control.

Ken jumped in. "You're up and doing well. We sprang this on Jack. I haven't even seen the orders or your chart yet. It's unfair to ask him to put a date on anything without the facts. Let us review the chart and orders and come back to you with a program."

"A week? That's insane." Jack directed his reply to Ken.

"I'm walking, driving and getting around just fine. The swelling is down in my back. A little strengthening is all I need," Lucas said.

"Is that what your doctor said or what you want to happen?" Jack walked over to him.

"I have a reputation to protect. The rodeo is my life. It's my money and my future. It's a lot of people's jobs as well, if ticket sales drop… I won't have people out of work. If I can't ride again, it makes people worry it's dangerous," Lucas explained.

"It is dangerous," Jack insisted.

"Jack," Ken said.

Bracing himself, Lucas knew Jack wasn't a wimp, a fan or a guy who'd fall in line. He was tough and Lucas liked it. Rodeo was dangerous but the trick of it was enjoying the danger. Playing the crowd. Lucas' whole life felt a bit like a performance—giving people what they wanted. He laughed off the challenge. "You've probably never ridden a horse in your life."

Jack shook his head. "You're wrong, Mr. Burr. I have ridden a horse. A nice tame horse that jumped fences and liked to be brushed—not a wild animal that was trying to throw me to the ground and stomp on me."

"Some men don't get it," Lucas said.

Jack's green eyes seemed even bigger. "Gay men or military men?"

"I didn't mean that," Lucas backpedaled. He didn't want to offend anyone. He'd always admired guys who were out and rode. Gay cowboys were popular with the ladies, but traditional old-fashioned rodeo guys mocked them. Texas was still full of old-fashioned types, its smaller towns especially. Lucas walked a fine line of tolerance and not pissing off the old guard.

"You know, when I worked the rodeo, I noticed not a lot of women riding. Why?" Jack asked.

"You just said it was dangerous," Greg pointed out.

"Of course, it is, but that's discrimination. If you want to risk your life riding bronc or bull, I don't care. Break your back or your neck and I'll be doing PT for you for the rest of your life in some capacity. Football, rodeo and old age keep me in business. But if women want to ride, I'm not sure I can work for someone who thinks women can't or shouldn't do the same things a man can," Jack said.

"Women do ride. They tend to do the barrel racing and other timed events. A couple of women have tried broncs but none have tried a bull. Let me clarify, no females have ever signed up to ride a bull, but they could if they wanted. Roping and racing have lots of ladies," Greg offered.

"Good. At least it's fair. I know I saw plenty of gay cowboys riding. Do you have a vet on site?" Jack asked.

"What?" Lucas jerked his head. He'd been distracted by the 'lots of gay cowboys' remark.

"A vet on site for the horses and bulls. They can be injured too," Jack said.

"All of the animals receive proper care and are cleared to perform," Greg replied.

"No vet on site at the rodeo." Jack looked down. "Everyone can do better."

"We have a kiddie rodeo group that's injury free and wildly popular. His momma runs it," Greg said.

"How sweet. And you have paramedics always on standby," he said.

Ken held up his hand. "We're here to help Mr. Burr, not tell him how to run his business."

Lucas locked eyes with Jack. "I agree a vet might be a good idea. I'm not giving up on rodeo because I got a little hurt. I don't like this judgment of my life and my work. You should help me whether I'm a republican or a democrat, a born Texan or a born Yankee."

"I will help you. I not judging you. I'm testing you. I know how to fix and handle your body better than you do. You ride rodeo and handle animals better than I could. You have to respect my expertise or this won't work. If you think you know medicine better than me or my colleagues, you're wasting my time and yours. Now, I do have a few questions that will help my assessment when I read the chart and orders." He sat back down.

"Shoot," Greg said.

"I want other options," Lucas replied. Facing the fall and its resultant publicity, Lucas had been fighting to get his reputation on top again. The fall had been worse than any other and he suspected someone was behind it, but no one would listen. Now he had a hot gay physical therapist talking about handling his body better? It was too much.

Greg shook his head. "This is the best place in Burrwood. If you go to a big city for treatment, then it'll be a story and not very loyal to your hometown."

"If it helps, I actually trained and worked in Dallas. I moved here to be near my aunt and uncle, when he got injured. He resisted PT but it's hard to talk back to your nephew. You won't get better treatment than me in the city," Jack reassured him.

Lucas smirked. "A helper or a bulldozer. I'm not looking for either."

"He's the best you'll get in all of Texas. Think of him as PT bootcamp. I'm sure you're tough enough to recover and be done with Jack," Ken insisted.

Greg turned to Lucas. "Lucas, consider it a challenge. Let's give them a chance to go over your chart. All your history—they'll see how tough you are. All those past injuries. What you can do in a short amount of time. Then we'll see what their plan is before you bail."

"Don't be afraid to get on the horse before you even try it," Jack teased.

Lucas locked eyes with the troublemaker. "I'd break you in no time."

That came out way flirtier and gayer than he'd intended. At least Lucas hadn't referred to Jack as a wild mustang, but that was exactly what Jack was like. Lucas found himself wanting to ride or tame Jack.

He took a deep breath and tried to get those pesky desires under control.

* * * *

Toward the end of the day, Jack finally got to sit down. Lucas Burr's chart had been authorized to his account and he sat in the break room reviewing it on a tablet.

"Finally." Bren walked in. "The residents were getting hangry."

Jack smiled. "They always finish before we do. They have their schedule of stuff and they never want to miss the activity before dinner because it puts them right there by the dining room."

"What are you working on?" Bren asked.

"Lucas Burr's chart. Rodeo men are insane," he said. Jack had to admit the pictures of Lucas' body were not bad to look at. The bruising had been extensive but now it was down to his back.

Bren chuckled. "Big money if they're good and good looking. He's both."

"He's a little arrogant and pushy too," Jack said.

"Pushy I could handle. Arrogant, well to climb on a wild bull—you gotta be at least a little crazy. Bet he's just as wild and crazy in bed." Bren winked.

"Good thing he's not your patient then. He's mine which means I need to keep it all strictly professional. I need to figure how to get him to listen and work with me. His back took a lot of pressure. The swelling and bulging discs are still aggravating him." Jack flipped through the series of scans and X-rays. Lucas was insanely hot and Jack had sensed something about him that made him want more. But he couldn't cross lines with a patient. "It's a miracle he didn't break his back."

"Those guys know how to take a fall. No broken arms or legs?" Brenda asked.

Jack shook his head. "Not even a rib. He's walking with a cane but nothing broken. Strong bones, I guess. We need to rebuild the strength in the back or he'll end up with slipped discs sooner rather than later."

"You'll whip him into shape," Bren said.

"I hope he'll listen. I've had tough patients before, but he wants to be riding in a week." Jack laughed.

"All you can do is tell him the risks. Get him to see it's smarter to do it right," Bren advised.

Jack smiled. "His body should tell him that. I'm not a miracle worker."

"Men hate to look weak in front of women, so it's better he has you, as much as I'd enjoy working him over." Bren frowned.

"We're all weak when we're injured. Worst case, if he can't handle a gay guy, Teddy can have him." Jack shrugged.

"Teddy would cave and get star struck," Bren said.

Jack nodded but before he could comment, Teddy rushed into the room.

"I found it," he said.

"Found what?" Jack asked.

Teddy pulled out his cell phone. "Burr's fall. The one that landed him in the hospital and here with you."

Jack watched the footage with interest. Knowing how Lucas fell could only help Jack formulate a treatment plan. Lucas' ass looked nice in those tight jeans and Jack couldn't help but admire the man's form and athletic skill.

His head and shoulders hit after, which was why he wasn't fully paralyzed or brain dead. His backside and lower back took the brunt of the force. "How in God's name did he not slip a disc in his lower back?"

Teddy took his phone back. "There are other angles." He flipped to the next video.

Bren leaned over. "He's a good-looking hunk of man."

Jack wouldn't dispute it. He wasn't too pretty and far from ugly, rugged and handsome. "And a tough one."

"He lost consciousness," Teddy pointed out.

"Briefly but you're right. Cell phones are scary good," Jack said.

Bren scoffed. "Never leave the house without hair and makeup, that was my mom's motto."

Teddy sighed. "This isn't about his looks or cameras. It's diagnostic."

"You're right. He never lost use of his arms. His legs were locked from the lower back due to swelling but he could always feel a tingling. Some docs had thought it was phantom but it had proved to be real. He got so lucky." Jack smiled. The viewing was for PT but looking at Lucas riding was hot—until he fell. Jack couldn't help but cringe.

Teddy switched to the next video.

"Look at that. The fall starts off looking like he's all over, but he gets control of himself. He landed straight and square on his back. Even a bit off and he would've slipped a disc or pinched one. His spine took the impact intact and compressed so it distributed the shock," Jack said.

"Rodeo hotties know how to take a fall and a hit." Bren blushed.

"Thanks, Teddy. This was really helpful. I had no idea people took their own video at rodeos." Jack shrugged.

"Got any footage of him riding before? Not falling?" Bren asked.

Teddy chuckled. "Plenty of that. I guess Lucas' people are trying to get the fall footage taken down, but it keeps popping back up."

"It's a public event and those people paid for their tickets," Bren replied.

"Publicity, they make a fuss to try and take it down only to draw attention to it." Jack waved it off.

"You don't think maybe Lucas's pride is hurt with people sharing video of him falling?" Bren asked.

Jack looked at his co-worker. "I think he might not like it but that manager of his is shrewd. Smart. He'll play all the angles to get the most publicity for as long as he can. Part of rodeo is celebrity. He wasn't rushing Lucas back on the bull—I think Greg is trying to milk the injury. Milk the fame for a big comeback. He's my best chance of keeping Lucas on the plan and not rushing to be back in the ring. Is that what it's called, a rodeo ring?"

Teddy laughed. "Yeah, that's it. You'll learn a lot more about roping and riding before you're done with Lucas, I'm pretty sure."

"I'd rope and ride him, any day," Brenda said.

"Have at it. Anything that keeps him in a good mood will help his sessions. But I doubt he could deliver in the bedroom right now. The strain and pain in his lower back…even if you're the one riding." Jack shook his head.

"I'll let him heal up a bit. I wouldn't want to make it look like you couldn't do you job by reinjuring him," Brenda teased.

"Thanks so much. I'm done for the day. I'll think on his treatment plan on the way home. Night, y'all," Jack said.

"Night," Bren called.

Teddy followed Jack out to the parking lot.

"What's wrong?" Jack asked.

Teddy blushed. "I follow Burr on Twitter. He said he'd be at a certain bar tonight, seeing what's up. Like he's back being normal. I thought maybe you'd like to go there. We can see how he's moving when he doesn't think medical people are watching. Others will be and maybe he's overcompensating, which makes the pain worse other times. Or maybe he's being honest, but we can blend in. He'd never see us."

Jack leaned on his car. "That sounds a lot like stalking a patient."

"No, it's on social media for all the public to see. That means the place will be packed but my cousin works there. He's going to save us a couple of seats or one of those tiny booths against the wall. We're just two colleagues having a drink and hanging out after a long day. Nothing weird and nothing to do with Lucas, as far as anyone else knows." Teddy smiled.

"I guess, I appreciate the effort, but I don't want him to get the wrong idea." Jack glanced at his rainbow tattoo. The attraction wasn't something Jack would admit but who wouldn't find Lucas hot? "Some guys get weird with a gay caretaker. I've had men request another therapist and some who tough it out. One even fooled me at first, acted like he was fine with it. Even acted like he liked me. Then when he was better, he filed a complaint that I'd touched him inappropriately," Jack shared.

"Inappropriately? Our job is to touch our patients," Teddy replied.

"I know. I think he said I touched his upper inner thigh too high up and he was uncomfortable. They paid off the patient, but it was dismissed internally. It was in Dallas—they had cameras all over from every angle and had independent reviewers look over every minute of treatment. They saw nothing that they would flag as inappropriate contact." Jack shook his head. If he had a patient that he wanted to be more than friends with and they felt the same, it was simple enough to move them to another therapist or wait until their treatment was done.

Being accused of touching some guy who Jack hadn't even been attracted to hurt. Some people just wanted to treat gays like predators or problems. Didn't they have better things to do?

"That sucks and everyone here knows and trusts you at work. Don't let your past mess with your head. I'm not saying ask the guy to dance. I know it's above and beyond, but if Lucas wants to be riding ASAP, you need to see how he's really moving. I'm willing to hang with you all night until he hobbles to his truck at last call. I wonder how sore and stooped over he'll be by then?" Teddy asked.

"I could snap a few of him not moving so well on my phone—just in case he pushes back too much. Proof he's not toughing through it all the time." Jack nodded. "Fine. Drinks are on me."

"Yes! My cousin, Mark, has been dying to meet you," Teddy said.

Jack sighed. It was more than a work field trip—it was a setup...another good excuse to be at this bar. Hopefully Mark was cute.

# Chapter Three

The Saddle-Up Saloon was always fun. Lucas Burr needed a dose of that after all the medical crap and people telling him what to do. He still had the nagging feeling that he'd been set up for this fall but wasn't about to whine in public about that.

Right now, Lucas needed to turn his brain off for a bit.

"You're sure about this?" Tim Hayes parked his pickup in the lot.

"I can have a few drinks. Find some pretty blonde to go home with. Prove I'm back in the saddle." Lucas nodded from the passenger side.

"Couldn't that sort of activity make your back seize up?" Tim asked.

"A tiny bit of pain for a lot of pleasure. What's wrong with that? We've both fallen—we've both had the aches and pains." Lucas opened the door and slid out.

*Carefully.* He'd never admit the constant pinch in his back or the ache running down his hips to his thighs. He forced himself to stand straight.

"Okay, at least you're not going to drink and drive," Tim said.

"Nah, definitely not with the pain pills." Lucas winked. "Joking. I'm not taking any damn pills. I'm tougher than that."

"If you need a ride home—"

Lucas shot Tim a look. "You think I'll strike out?"

Tim laughed. "Not a chance but a couple of line dances and you might be looking for an ice pack."

"I don't need to dance to catch a pretty lady. You're my wingman—plenty to go around." Lucas blew it off.

"Especially since you tweeted about it. Looks like you're craving attention," Tim replied.

Lucas used his cane but made it to the front door without limping too badly. "It looks like I'm back living life." If he had to put up with that flirty gay guy for PT, he would. But people would know he had a woman on his arm socially.

When Lucas walked in, the place erupted in applause and hoots and hollers.

Two prime seats waited for them at the bar. Lucas ordered two beers and the music could be heard as the noise of the crowd died down.

"How's the back?" the bartender asked Lucas.

"Getting better every day. Just another fall. I'll be back before you know it," Lucas said.

"The ladies missed you." The bartender grinned.

Lucas sipped his beer and glanced. Four lovely blonde ladies waited, staring him down.

But someone else caught his eye. A redhead in a small booth on the other side of the bar. That was Jack all right. Jack wasn't alone either—that football player

PT guy sat opposite Jack. They were chatting and laughing. Was it a date? Lucas knew Jack was gay but seeing him with someone else bugged him. Seeing him as a man—not just as a medical professional—made it hard to ignore the attraction.

"Mr. Burr," said one of the women behind him.

"Yeah." Lucas turned and smiled.

A couple of the girls were too young and he gave them autographs. He wasn't interested in jailbait. He had to play the part, the rodeo star who got all the women and hung out with his friends at the bar. Having a private dinner with friends or someone special would be better, but it wouldn't help his reputation. People wanted to see how much fun it was to be him. Fans lived vicariously through him…the thrills, the falls and the perks like the pretty ladies.

"I'm one semester away from my nursing degree, if you need any professional help," said a cool blonde with ice-blue eyes. She was slim and dressed like a daughter of Texas from hat to boots.

"Well, I'm doing just fine, but it never hurts to have healing hands around. What's your name?" Lucas asked.

"Lori," she said. "This is my friend, Tori. She's a massage therapist."

"Howdy to Lori and Tori. You know, Tori, my best friend Tim here has been very tense since my fall. He's a rider too, taken his falls, and he's tough but you always worry about your friends," Lucas said.

"That's so sweet." Tori put her hand on Tim's shoulder. "So tense."

With Tim occupied, Lucas let the nurse feel his spine. He tried to stay relaxed as she flirted with him. Her touch was gentle but he'd been pushing himself too hard to be pain free.

"You got out of the hospital so fast, it's impressive," Lori said.

Lucas grinned. "Thanks. Only tough guys last in rodeo."

"Very true. But you can't do it forever. You could end up in a wheelchair," Lori said.

That red hair caught his eye again. Jack had to be here for him. Burrwood was a small town with only six bars in it but he'd never seen Jack in here before. There was only one bar that catered to the LGBTQ+ crowd. What was Jack doing here?

"Hey, Mark," Lucas called to the bartender.

"Another round?" Mark asked.

"Get the ladies whatever they want. And a quick question." Lucas gestured for Mark to come closer and when Mark leaned in, asked, "That redheaded guy come in here a lot?"

The bartender looked in the direction Lucas was pointing. "Nope. He's here with my cousin, Teddy. First time I've met Jack. Physical therapist from Dallas, former military."

"Your cousin?" Lucas asked.

"Yeah, Teddy used to be a football player, college scholarship and all. But he got hurt bad enough to end his career. Positive guy though, he finished college and became a physical therapist. But he's going to be a trainer for a football team after he gets enough experience with all sorts of injuries…he volunteers with the high school teams and younger kids as a trainer. Great guy," Mark said.

Lucas nodded. "Nice. I just didn't recognize him from this angle."

"Oh, well, they're not reporters or anything. And if anyone bugs you, let me or Big Frankie know. He's working the door," Mark said.

"Thanks, good to know." Lucas didn't want anyone thinking he was paranoid but the press had been annoying.

He couldn't help but wonder why he was staring at his PT guy instead of the girls.

"Everything okay?" Lori asked.

Lucas forced a smile as his back grabbed his attention with another twinge. Bar stools were invented for the young and very strong of back.

"Everything is great. Do you enjoy the rodeo?" he asked.

She smiled. "I do. I was there when you fell. So scary. I rode horses when I was younger. I felt self-conscious about competing, but I enjoyed it."

"I can't imagine not riding horses. You know they have a mechanical bull in the back area?" Lucas asked.

"Are you getting on it?" Lori asked with a sparkle in her eyes.

"Not yet. My docs want me to go a bit slower. But if you want to show off, I'm happy to watch and give you feedback on your form," Lucas said.

Lori looked over. Tim and Tori were on the dancefloor. Lori nodded and shrugged. "Why not? Never got any negative feedback on my form."

She led the way and Lucas followed a bit slower than he wanted. He walked past the booth with Teddy and Jack and didn't even glance in their direction.

He leaned on the wall as Lori got in position, arching her back to show off her figure. She was very gorgeous, a grown woman—if a bit younger than him. His mother had been nagging him about settling down. The right woman would show up. That was what his dad had always said. That right woman would haunt a man until he realized she was what he needed, but he had to be quick because another man might snap her up.

Lucas paid attention, but he wasn't in a hurry. Sure, he'd like a son to pass it all down to and a little girl to show off in the kiddie parade. She'd be the best barrel racer on the circuit. But the right drop-dead gorgeous blonde had yet to show up.

He felt someone watching him and turned.

Teddy and Jack were standing a few feet behind him.

"Look who it is," Lucas said.

"Mr. Burr, this is a surprise. My friend and colleague, Teddy. Teddy, Lucas Burr, my new client," Jack introduced them with Texas manners and a satisfied smile.

The men shook hands. "Best wishes on your recovery," Teddy said.

"I'm just fine, thanks." Lucas studied Teddy. *Friend and colleague* screamed *not boyfriend*. But Teddy would be a good guy for Jack. Something told Lucas Teddy was on Jack's team.

"Your lady can certainly ride." Jack pointed.

Lucas turned and looked. "Yes, she can. What brings you here?"

Teddy smiled. "My cousin works the bar. We were just having an after-work drink."

"Nice. I thought you two might prefer another bar in town. Or be stalking me. Enjoy." Lucas smirked.

"Hardly stalking. I have your chart and I'm working on the plan. I'll see you in the office this week, if you're up for it," he said.

"Sure thing." Lucas heard a shout. "Excuse me."

He turned and saw Lori on the mats.

"If only the rodeo ring had such a cushioned floor," Jack teased.

"Excuse me." Lucas moved closer to the bull.

"We should get back," Jack said.

Lori looked like an angel even when freshly fallen off a mechanical bull. She hopped up and smiled, taming her hair. She got a coupon for a free appetizer and they headed to the bar to reclaim it. Fried cheese sticks were heaven and very unhealthy. Tori and Lori chatted about her bull riding.

"Doing okay?" Tim asked Lucas.

"That crazy PT guy is here. The redhead in the booth."

Tim looked. "Okay. What's the problem?"

"He's the only one who'll be trying to keep me from riding again in a week," Lucas said.

"You're not ready to ride. You're not ready to drive more than a short trip really," Tim scolded.

"I need to get back in the saddle soon. People need to see rodeo isn't that bad. That we're safe." Lucas downed the rest of his beer.

"We are safe, but you rushing in before you're ready will only be a bad example. You'll get hurt again or suffer another fall with injury. It's best to take your time,"

"That Jack has already wasted a few days prepping a plan. I want to be cleared and back to normal. He needs to get to work. It hurts the gate and the fans when something like this happens," Lucas explained.

"Paralysis is worse. Death is way worse. Take Lori home and have some fun, but don't overdo it. I want you back in the ring. It's no fun if there's no real competition,"

Lucas nodded. "You and Tori hit it off?"

Tim shrugged. "She's nice. I'm not looking for anything right now."

"Never hurts to try it out. See if it's something." Lucas smiled.

Tim shook his head. "Are you good to go with Lori?"

"Tonight at least. But I'm not thinking forever," Lucas replied.

He turned back to Lori and she held up the last cheese stick. Playfully, he took a bite.

She kissed him and pressed close. "Wanna come home with me?" she asked.

"I do," he said.

He shot a glance over at Jack. He and Teddy, the friend from work, were finishing up some potato skins.

"Everything okay?" Lori looked over.

"Absolutely. One thing with the bartender." Lucas leaned over the bar. "Mark, put your cousin and his friend's stuff on my tab."

"I've got it, Mr. Burr," Mark said.

"No, I appreciate that help with physical therapy. Good manners," Lucas said.

"Thank you, sir," Mark said.

"You paid for their stuff?" Lori leaned back. "Do you like gay men?"

Lucas smiled and hugged her to him. "No, I love blonde ladies. But they are part of my crack physical therapy team and they'll get me back on the bull in no time. Gotta treat your help right."

Lori kissed Lucas. "I like that. Let me help you back in the saddle." She fingered his belt buckle.

"We both like to ride," he agreed. Lucas had gotten used to the performance going into the bedroom. He knew the tricks to get himself to perform and now images Jack might end up part of that.

"Let's go. Sweep me off my feet, cowboy. I've only had one drink so I'm good to drive. I'm in the candy-apple-red pickup out front." She wrapped arms around his neck.

She lifted a leg like she expected him to carry her out of the bar.

A month ago, he'd have carried her and Tori together…one girl over each shoulder. No problem. But now—he wasn't there just yet.

"I wish I could but I'm still working on it. The bosses would be mad." Lucas cocked his head to Teddy and Jack.

"Well then you won't be much use even on your back." Lori grabbed her purse and Tori's hand. "We're out of here."

"Good luck. Mark, another round," Lucas said.

Tim shook his head. "We should go."

Lucas sighed. "Go on. I want another beer."

Tim nodded. "I thought you'd go home with her just for show even if your back isn't up to it yet."

"She wanted me to carry her. I couldn't have pulled it off without showing my weakness," Lucas said softly.

"A little time with that PT work and you'll handle every lady in town." Tim patted Lucas' shoulder. "I'll go smooth things over with Lori and Tori."

"Thanks," Lucas said. Tim was a nice guy—he'd probably take both girls home. Still, Lucas couldn't get his mind off Jack. He was fit and handsome as hell. Why couldn't he stop thinking about a guy? It'd happened before, rarely, but he drank it away. Girls were fun. He loved the adoration of women and the lack of judgment. Some of the women only liked him because he was a rodeo star or owned part of the rodeo. Some loved that he had money. If one woman didn't work out, there were always more groupies hanging out at the rodeo. He never treated them badly—every woman was a lady and someone's daughter—but if it didn't work out, it never seemed to bother him much.

Deep down, Lucas always enjoyed impressing other guys, his dad, his friends and especially certain guys who challenged him. Friendly competition and *boys will be boys* was fine—as long as his dad never caught him doing anything queer. Lucas remembered those comments cutting him. It was like his dad knew boys caught his eye more than girls.

Jack was bossy and shameless. He was confident and smart. In short, Jack was the sort of guy Lucas couldn't ignore—and here he was. There was a tiny gay back in town, why wasn't he there? It felt like Jack was taunting him.

Two beers later, Lucas felt no pain. His phone beeped a text from Tim.

*The girls are happy but you'll need to get a ride home…*

*NP…enjoy,* Lucas texted back.

Jack walked up. "Thanks for picking up the tab."

Lucas pushed the beer bottle away. "No problem. Can't wait to see you work your magic on me. My back…"

"My specialty. Need a ride home?" Jack offered.

"Nah, lots of ladies would be happy to," Lucas countered. "And you had a date, right?"

Leaning on the bar, Jack shook his head. "Not a date. He's a friend. Teddy took off. You might have plenty of offers but you're not ready to deliver in your condition. A few drinks and still in pain…those pretty little ladies won't be able to help you into bed."

"Is that what you want?" Lucas stared at Jack's rainbow ink. "To help me into bed?"

Mark shot Jack and Lucas a look.

"Not if you make it sound dirty. Professional help. If I'm going to get you back on the bull, I need you to not fall or hurt yourself. I also need you to trust me. I'm not going to hit on my patient. Straight or gay, no matter how hot the guy thinks he is." Jack smirked.

"Fine. Free ride home, I guess. I can afford a Lyft or whatever," Lucas defended.

"I'm sure, but they don't know how to safely move you or tuck you in," Jack teased. "Come on."

Lucas laughed. Jack nudged his elbow and he tensed. People might think Lucas was gay since he was hanging with Jack, but it was just professional. He wasn't some homophobe who couldn't handle the gay rodeo guys…some were very hot and the couples were cute. Still, small towns in the south were known to have groups of people dragging their heels and debating things on Sundays.

Sliding off the stool, Lucas felt Jack's hand on his arm. Why did it tingle? The blonde hadn't made him tingle like that.

"Too much beer," Lucas mumbled.

"I agree. I'd rather you take a pain pill as directed and limit yourself to one beer for social drinking," Jack said.

Lucas laughed. "So you're my boss now too. I have too many bosses. Greg, Mama and now you."

"I'm not your boss. I'm the one who can get you on the bull. If you really want to ride again, trust me." Jack squeezed Lucas' shoulder.

They made it out of the bar without a fall. Lucas followed along as Jack guided him to a white pickup truck.

Jack opened the door. "Can you trust me?"

Lucas sighed and looked into those green eyes. "How can I? All those girls want me. You're pretending you don't. I prefer blunt honesty."

Why did he want Jack to want him? Lucas stumbled over to a tree and puked up the last beer or three. He spit and shook his head. "Sorry. My tolerance seems to be lower since the hospital."

"Feel better?" Jack asked.

Lucas smiled. "I do. I'm not a drunk. I don't normally do that much except when—" Lucas stared at Jack and the heat made him confused. Lucas wasn't going to admit that most times with women he was drunk to some degree.

"When you want to avoid the truth or the pain?" Jack asked. "I get it. I can help. Hop in. I'll take you home and I promise, both hands on the wheel even though you are an attractive cowboy."

Lucas nodded but somewhere deep down, he was a bit disappointed Jack wasn't after him. Tiny hints of flirting weren't enough. Women were easy, but Lucas encouraged them. That was what cowboys were supposed to do. But men like Jack…he put his sexuality on his arm for all to see. So why wasn't he hitting on Lucas? Was it all the rodeo fame and maybe he wasn't as good-looking as he thought? Damn ego needed a boost, that was all there was to it. The women had helped and then deflated his ego just as quickly.

Maybe Jack was strictly professional, and the jokes and positive stuff was all part of the act? Lucas couldn't fault him for being professional, but did that mean the spark was all in Lucas' head? The desire wasn't mutual? His heart sank. So far, he'd liked talking to Jack. The nudges and the looks… There was something easy about being around him yet challenging at the same time. Jack would push him to be a better person, but maybe it was all about the physical therapy. Lucas was just another patient and Jack was a nice guy. Lucas getting his hopes up about the wrong guy might hurt more than that fall… He tried not to think about it.

He climbed into the truck and pulled on his seatbelt.

Driving Lucas home, Jack found himself torn. He was attracted to the cowboy, with his tight round ass, the tall lanky muscle, like a swimmer, only rougher.

But he was a professional. He was also not into chasing straight guys who were curious or closet cases. Unfortunately, the pool of openly gay men was mostly taken, younger, older or sparkless—for Jack at least. Teddy's cousin Mark was nice, but it was nothing like the electricity for Jack with Lucas.

He'd watched every time a girl tried to climb Lucas or stick her tongue in his mouth. Was Jack jealous? Worried about his patient? It was weird.

"You're quiet there," Lucas said.

"Figured you'd have a headache, not want to talk," Jack replied.

Lucas leaned on the door. "I don't know why you picked me. Mark's a good bartender, nice guy—he'd have gotten me a ride. Didn't know he was gay. He should work at that other bar. The Rainbow Rose…yeah, that's it."

"Why?" Jack asked. The fact that Lucas knew the name of the only—tiny—gay bar in town surprised Jack but he didn't let that register on his face. Lucas was a puzzle. Was he really into all these women groupies? He seemed to be, but celebrity had its own set of rules… Jack had worked with some big celebrities in Dallas, NFL stars who admitted it was hard to be nice when you were hurt, tired or just traveled out. The fans, however, wanted a smile, a selfie, an autograph and the players never wanted to disappoint. Some were jerks but most knew popularity was as important as their part on the team. Even after they retired, they could trade on their celebrity if they'd built it up enough.

And Lucas owned part of the rodeo and a big ranch. The guy had money and good prospects. Those girls weren't dumb to go after him. Why did Jack ache to get past the celebrity façade and know what Lucas really wanted? Lucas the man, not the celebrity or the cowboy.

"Why not go to the gay bar? Girls hit on Mark all the time. Odds are better at the other bar if he wants a guy. You too. Oh, but if Teddy was setting you up with Mark, then you have to go where Mark is. That makes sense," Lucas reasoned.

"Mark will be there. It's a small town—people are easy enough to find. You're my patient and I don't want you to further injure yourself. A setback could hurt my reputation and your career," Jack teased.

Lucas laughed. "I guess it's high stakes for both of us."

"Rodeo guys don't always come in for PT. Most of them are young and just bounce back or tough it out. If we can get your trust, maybe we'll get the rodeo business and those guys will heal up better from their injuries with fewer long-term issues. Win-win." Jack stopped at a stop sign. "Which way?"

Lucas navigated. "You don't have a boyfriend?"

Jack shook his head. "Nah, waiting for the right one."

"You're not hooking up with Teddy or Mark? Any of the guys at the gay bar?" Lucas asked.

"I hooked up plenty in the military and college. It's fun—don't get me wrong—but if you don't build a relationship, it sort of feels pointless after a bit. Plenty of hot guys in the world and they're around when you need a dose of sex or ego boost. I guess there comes a point when sex isn't enough—you want someone who wants you all the time not just naked." Jack shrugged.

"Hot guys anytime you want and it gets old? I don't believe it," Lucas scoffed.

Was Lucas talking about Jack's life or his own fantasies? Jack knew Lucas wasn't totally drunk off his ass but it was confusing. "You never get tired of the groupies? You never want to shut out that side of things and just be with someone who knows you and you don't have to put on an act? Then again, you don't seem too sad that that girl didn't work out," Jack said.

"Cuz of the injury," Lucas said through gritted teeth and pointed a finger in Jack's shoulder. "I'll be back to normal in a week or two. Thanks to you."

"Are you in pain?" Jack asked.

"No, I'm not—but that much fun might've strained something. Picking up that girl would've been too much. Over your limit of what I could lift, I'm sure. You know, I've had plenty of gay rodeo guys hit on me in my career. Pissed off my dad whenever they came around when I was a teen. He thought I was encouraging them or something. I don't know what the deal is," Lucas said.

"You're a good-looking guy. Why not try? Not everyone gets a tattoo or has perfect gaydar. Some people like both and that's okay too if you're just looking for a hookup. Your dad sounds like he's a piece of work." Jack chuckled.

"He died but he was old-school. Hardcore. Get hurt, rub some dirt on it, walk it off." Lucas smirked.

"My dad isn't quite that rough. He doesn't know what to say sometimes with the gay stuff so he stays quiet," Jack said.

"And college and everything was just fine and happy?" Lucas asked.

"The military wasn't fine. I got tired of being asked and harassed in the military. You wanna fight me over it, do it. Don't talk behind my back. That's why I got the tattoo. It made college a lot of fun without drama or questions," Jack said.

"I get that. People talking behind your back sucks. I get a little celebrity in a small town and it's great until you fall or step in the wrong direction. Then everyone is talking. What did I do wrong when I fell? When will I be back? Will I retire? Was I drunk?" Lucas sighed.

"Were you drunk?" Jack asked.

Lucas punched the dashboard. "No, I don't ride like that. I swear, that bull was drugged or something. It was like it was lame in one leg and jerking like crazy. One leg was off. I've ridden for decades and never felt a bull like that. So much energy but favoring a leg."

"Sorry, I saw the video and the bull was moving fast. I didn't see an injury," Jack replied.

"I know that. I was on the damn thing. I felt it startle and shift right before the start. Someone might've cut him, but I didn't see any blood in the video. It's like someone spiked the bull. The movements weren't all natural. I've been riding since I was a kid. I know when something is off." Lucas pointed. "Turn in there. The first little house on the left."

The house was hardly small—a two-story brick home with wraparound porch and plenty of shade trees. It looked ideal.

Jack parked the truck, turned to Lucas and nodded. "I believe you."

Lucas stared at him intently. "Liar. You just want the business. You want me to cooperate and make you a name."

Jack put his hand on Lucas' knee. "No. I'm the best because I'm the best. If you say something was off with the animal, it was off. Let's look at the footage…all that we can find. If someone sabotaged you, they need to face justice. Tampering with an animal is abuse. But none of that will go back in time and fix your back. You have to trust me and work the program I set up. Deal?"

Lucas looked at the hand on his knee. "Deal. I just don't want people to think that—"

Jack removed his hand. "No one will think you're anything more than my patient. That's all you are."

"Thanks for the ride." Lucas opened the door.

Jack got out and rounded the truck. Lucas stumbled a bit but stayed upright. He was still a bit drunk, tired and sore.

"I'm fine," Lucas insisted.

"I can walk you to the door. I'd be a terrible date if I didn't. You did buy my drinks and apps," Jack teased.

Lucas looked at Jack and snorted a laugh. They managed the stairs and Lucas opened the door. "It's just the guesthouse. No one is in here. I sleep off a few drinks or bring guests here, mama doesn't need to know."

Following Lucas, Jack admired the two-story home. It was cozier than the large ranch compound had looked when Jack had turned down the drive. That main house was dead ahead but quite a ways down the road and five times the size. A proper Texas spread.

Lucas walked to the bathroom and Jack followed, Lucas rinsed his mouth with water and then mouthwash. "All better. I'll crash on the couch."

"Is that good for your back?" Jack asked.

"Better than the stairs. The bedrooms are upstairs except for the office—that has a pull-out sofa but the mattress isn't great. You'd never approve." Lucas turned and poked Jack in the chest. "Are you trying to get me into bed?"

"Yes, that's the idea." Jack grinned.

"You could've taken me to your place. I wouldn't object," Lucas said.

Was this flirting? Jack wasn't sure what he'd gotten himself tangled up with in this cowboy. "My apartment is on the third floor with just stairs so you'd feel that. Not great for you if you don't want to go to the second floor here. Would the main house be better?"

"No, no." Lucas leaned on Jack's shoulder. "My mother is there and we'd wake her up. And her dog. So many questions and I don't like to worry her. That's why I bring hot girls here. Not that you're a girl. Wow, that sounded bad. But you are hot. I'm sure you know that already." Lucas stared at Jack for a quiet moment.

Jack wasn't sure if he was about to be kissed or punched. "It's okay. I get it. I moved from Dallas and the distance from my parents really helped. Your dad being dead, you don't want to abandon your mom, but you want some privacy."

"Exactly. I'll be fine." Lucas patted Jack's chest. "You could ride. You've got the muscle for it. Most of the cowboys are leaner, but the more muscle, the more a bull has to throw off." Lucas' hand lingered.

"The military was enough of an adrenaline rush for me. I'm not interested in rodeo. That's your thing." Jack was pretty sure Lucas was flirting or trying to on some level. He wasn't that drunk anymore, but he was hanging in the deniability zone. If Jack made a move, Lucas could claim he'd misread the situation. Jack knew Lucas wasn't going to hurt him, but denial was a powerful thing when people bought into it fully. Some guys tried to get real, only to freak out and blame the gay guy for making a move. Jack wasn't going to play games.

More importantly, this was a patient. Jack wasn't going to screw around no matter what.

"Is it? I'm not sure how long… I'll be fine." Lucas waved it off and gestured to the couch.

"Fine." Jack went into the kitchen. He poured Lucas a big glass of water and found a small trash can tucked under the sink.

Back in the living room, he set the water on the coffee table and the empty can by the side of the couch. "Get some sleep. I'll call you in the morning and we can set up your first appointment," Jack said.

"Okay." Lucas stood up and followed Jack to the front door.

"No, you're supposed to get on the couch so I know you're safe for the night." Jack turned and nudged Lucas back.

"I'm fine. You're a good guy. I wanted a woman physical therapist because women are so nurturing. It's okay to have a woman take care of you. I hate looking weak in front of guys." Lucas patted Jack on the shoulder.

"None of my patients are weak. They're all recovering from what life does to us. But I get it. No harm done, but you're stuck with me." Jack nodded to the couch. The *weak* thing clicked in Jack's brain. He'd seen it hundreds of times with concerned wives. The husbands let them cook, clean, do all the laundry and so on—and they fussed over their guy coming to PT. The men would act like they didn't need it, but it was a break from the wife or to make her happy. In front of men, they bragged that they had the wife taking care of them and they were just fine. They'd be done with PT if only the doc would sign off or work would let them back. Like they were superheroes stronger than any other guy there.

Jack smiled at Lucas. He had a better idea of how Lucas' mind worked. "Get some rest. I won't be easy on you in PT."

"Night," Lucas said.

As Jack opened the screen door, Lucas pulled him back. "You'll really help me figure out if someone messed with the bull?"

Jack smiled. "Sure, I'll try. I've got a dog at home. I don't like the idea of someone hurting any animal."

"What kind of dog? My dad never let us have a dog in the house. They were ranch dogs." Lucas leaned on Jack.

"We can talk about that tomorrow. You need to hydrate and get some sleep. We'll talk dogs and bull conspiracies during the workout." Jack patted Lucas' arm.

Lucas didn't let go—he leaned in. Jack braced Lucas' shoulders but the kiss rocked him back on his heels. Straight-cowboy drama wasn't something he'd signed up for but Lucas probably wouldn't remember it. The guy could kiss so Jack indulged for a few seconds. When Lucas tried to pull Jack in and started using tongue, Jack had to dial it back and guide him to the couch or he'd get into a situation that would get him fired. He wanted to play with Lucas, even if it was just a single night of fun, but that would have to wait until Lucas was sober and they were done with PT.

"Get some sleep." Jack pulled an old quilt from the back of the couch over on Lucas and that seemed to settle him down.

Jack slipped out of the house and looked around. The compound might have security. Or some rabid fans could be hiding behind the trees. Things had gotten weird but if history was any proof about confused straight guys on the down low, Lucas would only bring it up in private. No word of Lucas in the gay bar or hooking up with guys in Burwood had ever reached Jack so he wasn't out as bi or anything else—he was keeping this side of himself quiet.

Jack relished the memory on the ride home.

He just had to act normal with Lucas from now on and try not to fantasize about that cowboy.

# Chapter Four

Lucas had control of himself everywhere but in his dreams. Even that stupid kiss was a safe move. At least it'd felt safe. Jack was a good guy.

In his dreams, things went further and Lucas couldn't stop himself. On that old plaid couch, he and Jack made out like teenagers. Shirts flew off and flies opened. Jack's hand was magic on Luca's dick but Lucas was the instigator. He licked his way down Jack's well-defined chest to his thick and tempting erection.

No words, no confusion about what he was or wanted. No shame, no fear—he sucked Jack off, teasing and taking his time. Jack's hand pushing Lucas' head down made him smile. Instead of going faster, he licked slowly from balls to tip and flicked his tongue until Jack gripped his hair. They could linger and enjoy without rushing.

The few times he'd hooked up around the horse trailers of the rodeo, it was always quick and trying to avoid being seen. One time, Lucas had been extra wrong, so wrong. The guy had been looking for tips, tricks and insider help. A mega fan trying to make friends to use Lucas for connections and interest. Trevor, that guy haunted him. They'd had a few beers one night and Lucas had misread the situation completely—he'd made a move and Trevor had freaked out. Lucas made it out with a black eye and nearly broken jaw.

Was that why Jack was so easy? He was fully out and there was no doubt. Lucas inhaled Jack's scent and let their mutual heat melt any reservations. He wanted Jack for Jack, but no guessing games made it so much hotter for him.

Lucas gave in and swallowed that cock all the way down, sucking Jack until he came. Instead of a sweet reward, Lucas woke up alone with a hard on pinned in his tight jeans.

"Why? Why him?" Lucas muttered to himself.

Lucas had always tried to be more open-minded than his dad. The old guard made it hard for the gay cowboys around, especially in a small town. Lucas had witnessed it on the rodeo circuit. Those cowboys always lived in the big cities.

He'd never understood the problem until he'd watched a couple cowboys making out. It was sparking feelings but his dad had caught him watching and beaten the crap out of him.

Later, when his dad had told him it was wrong, Lucas had said he was just confused by what he saw.

Lucas had an easy time charming the girls and he liked the attention. It wasn't a lie. Checking out the competition was part of the job so he got to admire men without a problem. Part of him always wrote off the attraction as wanting to defy his father and be better. Be fair, kind and tough. That was for more enlightened than his father's mantra of what made a man—plenty of beer, pussy and money.

Lucas had plenty of female admirers and most of them bought his act. A few were experienced and aggressive but he usually played off the gentleman card well enough to catch up. He'd never forget the first woman who'd called him on his wandering gaze. Suzie had been an older woman and loved the cowboys, and she'd been watching him during a line dance at a bar. Lucas enjoyed the attention but his eye had always shifted to the guy beyond her.

When he'd finally asked her to dance, she had, but Suzie had asked about the guy, not Lucas. Were they old friends? Rivals? Enemies? Lucas had played dumb, swearing he'd only been looking at her. She'd started whispering in Lucas' ear about how hot that guy was and what she'd do to him. It'd gotten a rise out of Lucas and she'd claimed she'd won a bet.

Nothing like that terror to put a guy back in the closet far enough to find his mama's high school prom dress. She and the guy had never said anything—at least nothing that had gotten back to Lucas—but still the fear that someone could see through him so easily made him hide and deny harder.

Occasionally he found a guy who caught his eye and made his sleep more interesting. He'd never acted on it. Drinking usually dulled the feelings, which had been the plan last night. Only the problem guy had shown up at the same bar—and driven him home.

Lucas wanted to kick himself. He had to work with this guy on his injured back. Now what? None of this was Jack's fault but Lucas couldn't— He had to sweep it under the rug and focus on his recovery.

His phone rang and Lucas reached for it, his back tightening up. He had texts from Greg and his mom was calling. The guest house was his refuge but it wasn't much of a secret. At least they didn't show up and really embarrass him.

He hit the bathroom then exited the guest house. If only Tori or Lori had been more understanding last night, he might not be in this awkward mess—but they wanted the rodeo star, not the real guy.

* * * *

"Residents again!" Brenda complained only when Ken was completely out of earshot.

Teddy rolled his eyes. "You know Jack has got Burr all morning. He's the special project. What did you expect?"

"Fine, sure. Good luck with your handful," Brenda teased.

Jack sipped his coffee. "Thanks. Have fun making the rounds."

Once Brenda had stalked off in a mini huff, Jack shook his head. "I like her but she thinks everything should be handed to her. Like we're going to offer to swap assignments!"

"Her daddy owns a couple of car dealerships. I'm shocked she works for anyone else," Teddy said.

Jack shrugged. "I bought my truck from them when I moved to Burrwood. Did all my online research and they didn't gouge me so I can't hate them for that. Maybe Brenda prefers the medical field. I couldn't sell cars."

"Maybe she's looking for a doctor hubby?" Teddy wondered.

"She'd be better off as a nurse or medical assistant in some office. Or anything in a hospital. Here, we're not really doctor central," Jack said.

"You know she changes the channel in the patients' rooms to her trashy talk shows," Teddy added.

"Gossip gets you nowhere," Jack advised.

"Not gossip if it's true. I do my share of patient rounds. One lady just wanted her game shows to stay on. She worked harder that way. I get it, some of those old coots want their conservative news shows on but I'll listen to anything if gets them to focus on the work." Teddy filled his water bottle.

"I'm glad you're with me today. I might need backup with Lucas." Jack hated asking for help, but Teddy was a good guy.

"Sure. Mark was kind of bummed that you took Lucas home, but I told him it was for your work. I'll set up another meeting for you two, when he's not swamped working. What do you need today? Burr is an intimidating cowboy. I think you'll handle him just fine." Teddy grinned.

Jack filled his own water bottle and checked the clock on the wall. Nearly time to open. Not judging people was rule number one and he'd judged Lucas quite a bit already. He was grumpy and in pain but him drinking and picking up women was none of Jack's business.

The drinking might be, but Jack had rechecked his chart. Burr had refused opioids of any kind and was making do on anti-inflammatories and OTC painkillers. He was tough and rich but he didn't act like an entitled ass…at least not most of the time.

What was the real Lucas like? Brenda showed her true colors around her peers. She had a new car every model year and it was top of the line. Lucas kept his truths to himself. Jack could relate. He hadn't needed a new car when he moved from Dallas, but the high-end SUV he had gotten from his parents as a graduation gift sent the wrong message in small town Burrwood. A well-equipped Toyota pickup went unnoticed but a base Lexus SUV—that label caught people's attention and judgment.

In Dallas, that message mattered to his parents. Jack liked living where it wasn't necessary to prove something—other than that he was a decent guy and good at his job.

He walked out front and set up the area. His whole morning was Lucas Burr. Teddy booted up the computer, since Lexi didn't come in for another half an hour. Jack headed for the front door, unlocked it then switched the sign to show that they were open.

Greg and Lucas were there already. Greg nudged Lucas.

"Good morning." Jack put on his best positive attitude.

"Good morning, Jack. Here he is, bright eyed and bushy tailed," Greg said.

"Thank you. You can pick him up at noon," Jack said.

Greg nodded. "I'm going to shoot the breeze with Ken for a while. If you need me."

"Your babysitter seems nice," Jack teased.

"He's just looking for any excuse to goof off and BS. If Ken keeps Greg from worrying and overreacting, that's fine with me." Lucas sat on the bench. "What's first?"

"First, I should thank you for buying Teddy and my drinks at the bar the other night. That wasn't necessary," he said.

"No, but a nice gesture. If you're going to stalk me, you'll have to hide better than that." He smirked. "But I should thank you for the ride home. All good with the Texas manners?"

Jack liked the sparkle in his eye. He'd been caught but he'd never admit it. "Good for me."

"No nagging about my drinking?" Lucas shot back.

"If you're really not taking the pain pills prescribed, I won't. But getting drunk only ups your chances for a fall, so dial it back, please. You know it's okay to take a little oxy when you really need it, but don't mix it with other things. Just limit the alcohol and taper down," Jack advised.

He shook his head. "I overdid it last night, I'm sorry. I don't normally do that. But I don't normally have trouble picking up a pretty lady, physically. I could've taken her home but I'm not my old self yet with a fireman's carry."

"Agreed. Don't do that at all until you're totally recovered. We'll get you there but you don't have to prove anything to anyone until you're ready." Jack looked into Lucas' deep brown eyes for any inkling of the line he'd crossed. Jack couldn't forget the passion behind that spontaneous kiss.

"I saw what binge drinking did to some friends. I hauled their asses to rehab. No one is having to do that for me. It's a one-off here and there," Lucas said.

"This therapy will work you. It will hurt after. Are you sure you might not want to get that oxy script filled just in case you need it after?" He didn't want this guy to suffer or turn to booze—though another kiss wouldn't be the worst thing.

Lucas seemed like he had the will to stop when it was time. Jack respected that. Admired it. Maybe he wasn't all ego?

He shook his head. "I don't want the temptation around. I'm using over-the-counter pills to take the edge off, beer as needed."

"A true cowboy. Okay, stand up. Let's get a handle on your range of motion. Tell me when it hurts." Jack manipulated Lucas' arms in every way.

Lucas didn't say a word and his body never tensed or pulsed in any way to signal pain. Jack turned Lucas' head. His skin was warm and tan, like he spent a lot of time in the sun. He smelled like leather and horses.

"Have you tried riding at all?" Jack asked.

"Didn't think that was okay," he replied.

"Probably not yet. But you've been around horses?" He didn't want to accuse him of lying, but the smell was hard to miss. Not a bad smell like he'd stepped in manure but that hint of real ranching.

"I own a big old ranch. You only saw the guest house last night. I got hands to work the fences and tend all the animals but I have to visit the stables. Horses know their owners. They get twitchy when you change their routines. Hands are riding them. I fed the chickens too—can you smell them, Colonel?" he shot back.

Jack laughed. "I didn't mean anything by it. But some patients don't follow the rules. I need to know if I can trust you."

Lucas frowned. "I'm a man of my word. I said I'd give you a try out, and here I am. I assume you're a man of your word?"

"A try out?" Jack pressed on Lucas' back. "Bend over and try and touch your toes."

He bent and winced.

"Pain?" he asked.

"A bit," Lucas admitted.

Jack felt along his spine. "Okay. Stand up. Straighten out your hips."

"They're straight," Lucas said.

Jack heard whispers. Looking over, some of the other patients who were part of Teddy's knee replacement group were chatting.

"Team therapy only works if you're working," Jack called.

Teddy took over and coached them.

"You like being bossy." Lucas locked eyes with Jack.

"I realize you're a local celebrity and people might talk or take note. We can get a private room if you prefer, but there's more room to move out here," he said.

"Local? You like taking shots," he snarked.

Jack frowned and put his hands on Lucas' hips, exerting pressure on the one that was hiked up a bit. "I'm trying to protect your privacy, is all."

He grunted. "That pain was all from you."

"You're favoring one side. You can't." He held him despite the pain.

"Everyone does. Right- or left-handed, it's natural. You have a dominant side, as a rider. It's not going to be undone by you," he warned.

"That's what gives a cowboy his swagger? We'll see about that." Jack let him go and Lucas winced.

Jack smiled to himself and went for a piece of equipment.

"You like making people suffer?" Lucas asked.

"No, I like making them stronger. Pain is part of healing. If all you needed were stitches, those would still ache and itch. New skin has to grow and there might be a bit of a scar. But your injuries are on the inside. The pain is proof we're working on the right spots. Rebuilding your strength and control," he explained.

"I think you like it. Maybe it's the perfect job for you? Touching men and making them hurt. Maybe you should just open some weird dungeon. Probably make a lot more money?" He sat down.

Jack stifled a laugh. Lucas was in pain but the idea of Jack running a dungeon…was this more weird cowboy flirting?

"Is that what you like? Pain and men bossing you around?" Jack teased.

Lucas shook his head. "No, I was just giving you a hard time."

"Good. I get pain is part of your job but with this sort of injury, the pain is real and you have go through it to get strong again. That means you'll feel worse before you feel better, that's how it works," Jack lectured.

Teddy walked over. "Can we please keep the dom kinky whatever talk down around the over-sixty set? We've got church folks that come here, Mr. Burr," Teddy scolded.

"Sorry about that." Lucas nodded to Teddy.

Jack took a deep breath. "Believe it or not, I'm trying to help. I thought we were doing okay. But if you can't handle a little teasing when you gave it to me outright… Let's start over?"

Lucas eyed Jack up and down. "I want to do this my way."

"Your way? *You* went to school for physical therapy?" he asked.

"I know my limits and what I can do. But nagging isn't motivational," he said.

"Nagging? Questions and instructions aren't nagging—it's my job. You have a problem with me," Jack said.

Lucas froze and the look in his eye was cold as ice. "I love women. Blondes with big blue eyes and good figures who are fun."

Jack smiled—so Lucas did remember what he'd done. It wasn't the best idea but Jack hadn't initiated anything. This was his patient. No matter how attracted to Lucas Jack was, he had to be professional. He always got a little involved in the lives of his patients—what they needed and how they lived impacted their goals. Jack couldn't let the lines blur. "Fair enough. Why don't we go into the private room and I'll show you some exercises you can do on your own?"

Lucas followed. "You just want me alone."

Jack closed the door behind them. "You're the one who made me promise to help with the potential animal abuse or doping. You want that to be the talk of the town?"

"Sorry, no. I thought… I didn't think you'd follow through with it. People never really believe I need help with anything." Lucas shook his head.

"Believe it or not, I'm a man of my word too. Let's get another thing straight. You kissed me. I wasn't going to bring it up because you were drunk, and maybe you didn't remember it, but fine, it's out there. You did it, not me. I'm not someone who takes advantage of someone who is intoxicated or is a patient of mine," Jack warned.

"It was all the alcohol and build-up. It wasn't about you," Lucas said.

Jack didn't believe that for a minute but if it saved them both some embarrassment, fine. He scoffed and pulled out a sheet of exercises from his folder on Lucas. "Okay."

"No, not laugh it off okay. I like women," Lucas said firmly.

"I like women too, as friends. I know what my deal is. Yours, that's up to you to figure out," Jack replied.

"I'm straight. Women are my deal." Lucas dropped his cane. "I thought you were on my side."

"I am. You're the one getting frustrated. I'll help you with PT and looking into the 'who set-up your accident' thing, I promised. But I never laid an unprofessional hand on you and I won't. You crossed that line," Jack pointed out.

Lucas nodded. "Fair enough. I'm sorry."

"You don't need to be sorry. I'm not offended, but, while you're my patient, that could get me fired or at least suspended and written up. I'm not the answer to your issues. Maybe you're bi," Jack reasoned. That would explain Lucas' confusion—if he liked it with women, then why the pull toward anything else? Sometimes life was complicated.

"No, I'm not bi," Lucas insisted.

"I believe you." Jack smiled and moved in closer. He pressed the sheet of paper full of exercises to Lucas' chest. "Then keep your lips off me. Now let's try some of these exercises so you can do them right at home."

"I have the videos of the ride on my phone. Just tell me the truth. If I'm wrong, I'm wrong. Everyone keeps saying a bad fall is just a matter of time. I should just shake it off." Lucas handed over his phone and unlocked it.

"It is—your odds of being injured go up the longer you do this work, but things factor in. You have someone screw up the rope ties or let the animal go with a painful abscess on a hoof and the animal will be even more dangerous," Jack agreed.

He watched Lucas start one of the exercises with good form. Then Jack watched a video or two. "The bull is favoring one side. Don't vets have to sign off?"

"We can go to the rodeo and check on who the vet was that cleared the bull. Make sure the paperwork is in order," Lucas said.

"Won't we need a warrant or something?" Jack asked.

Lucas smiled. "I own a quarter of that rodeo. I can see the records and the books any time I want."

"Let's do it," Jack agreed. This side mission of finding the truth out about Lucas' fall was only going to make the attraction harder to fight. Jack had self-control, but if Lucas kept coming at him the way he had—so hungry and sure—Jack wasn't at all confident that he could resist.

# Chapter Five

"Does this happen a lot? Sabotage? I mean rivals in the rodeo, I understand, but trying to hurt another rider seems—like really asking for something bad to happen to you," Jack said.

Lucas shrugged. "I agree. We do have some cases of tampering with equipment or trying to get another rider drunk. Usually it doesn't involve the animals, though."

Lucas parked his truck at the rodeo office doors and realized it might be odd to have Jack tagging along the whole time on the investigation. He liked the idea of Jack's help but if people saw them going around everywhere together… "You don't have to go in."

"What? Why am I here then?" Jack asked.

"Fine. I don't want people to get the wrong idea. You could lose out on that Mark guy," Lucas defended.

"I have plenty of friends, gay, straight, bi and so on. If Mark or any guy I might date has a problem with me being friends with someone, it won't work." Jack opened the door.

Lucas led the way inside the office. A middle-aged woman sat behind the desk. She smiled big when she saw Lucas.

"Hi, Donna, this is my friend Jack who is helping with my PT. We wanted to see the files on the bull I rode that night. Make sure all the papers were in order," Lucas said.

"Nice to meet you, Jack." Donna nodded. "No problem. There was no problem with the paperwork, but of course you can see it."

She flipped through a filing cabinet and pulled out a file. "Here you go, signed and dated. Vet was Doc Maddox. Nothing unusual. If you want to review it in the spare office, it's free. Or make copies—the copy machine got moved in there with the fancy new coffee station. Coffee?"

"No, thanks," Jack said.

"None for me but we'll look it over and make some copies. Thanks, Donna." Lucas winked.

"Let me know if you need anything else," she said.

Lucas led the way to the spare office and locked the door behind Jack.

"You've got a lot of fans," Jack teased.

Lucas took a deep breath. Being alone with Jack was what he wanted but also a dangerous temptation. "She's married with two kids. Those are the kinds of fans I like."

Jack frowned. "No special girl."

"Don't, please don't bring up...we're here for proof or clues," Lucas insisted.

"Of course. I'm not sure how to help." Jack sat in the desk chair and flipped open the file.

Lucas leaned over Jack, enjoying the fresh and masculine scent of him. "What does that even say?"

Jack smirked. "I'm good for something. I can read doctor scribble. Let's find the right date. Here we go. Bull is called Mad Max and the vet is Dr. Maddox. The owner is Lou Paxton. Vet says bull is up-to-date on all shots and shows no sign of illness, infestation, pests, injury or pain that would prevent Mad Max from entering the ring."

Leaning over, Lucas shook his head. "Nothing?"

"Is Maddox a reliable vet? Maybe someone bribed him?" Jack suggested.

"I don't use him personally. He's pretty old but he likes to feel like he's the old guard and everyone feeds his ego. We should probably visit him and see if he gets nervous about us asking questions." Lucas grabbed the folder and copied the relevant pages.

Jack walked over next to him and put a hand on Lucas' arm. "Maybe it's a mistake? Maybe the old guy needs new glasses and missed something? We should check the bull too."

"That will be a bit trickier. They travel to other rodeos so we're not always riding the same animals. Keeps it fresh." Lucas turned and was inches from Jack.

"You'll figure it out, find the time. I like playing Nancy Drew." Jack smiled.

Lucas stared at Jack's arm and pushed up his sleeve to see the ink. "Does it ever bother you? Ever wish you hadn't?"

"Does it bother you?" Jack asked.

Lucas sighed. "It's your body. But it's Texas, it's the south. It's something for people to judge you on."

"You don't like my body?" Jack teased.

Lucas's blood boiled. "You're just baiting me."

"You brought it up. I don't have a ton of ink." Jack pulled up his other sleeve then lifted the hem of his shirt. "Just the ones on my upper arm. Below the waist, well you'd have to find out for yourself." Jack let the shirt drop.

Lucas wanted to rip off Jack's clothes. "Do you like playing this game?"

Jack moved in a bit closer. "You started it. You get nervous and stare at me. I'm not playing anything. I'm attracted to you. I like you. Cocky rodeo cowboy and all."

"Playing with a straight guy like you want to be his boyfriend isn't fair," Lucas said.

"You can think whatever you want but I haven't done that. Not even close. If I was your boyfriend, I'd say please don't ride bull or broncs ever again. I don't want to see you hurt or in a wheelchair." Jack smiled.

"I'd recover. Falls happen," Lucas said.

Jack pressed to Lucas and reached an arm around. He slid his hand down Lucas's spine and settled, pressing gently on an area that didn't hurt. "Here—if you break your back around here—odds are very good that your legs won't work and your dick won't work."

Leaning in a bit, Lucas needed more. The heat seemed to meld them together as Jack's fingers innocently taunted Lucas' back.

"Bad enough never to be able to walk again but not to be able to get it up? Feel that release? I enjoy getting screwed as much as screwing but to never get hard again—that's not worth the risk," Jack said.

Lucas chuckled. "We risk it every time we're in a car."

"Come on. Your bull doesn't have airbags, seatbelts, crumple zone or, hell, even a steering wheel. I get it, you love the adrenaline, but you could find something else to motivate you. I'd want you to—if you were my boyfriend." Jack dropped his hand from Lucas' back and moved away slightly.

Lucas grabbed Jack by the back of the neck and kissed him fiercely. Jack kissed him back and Lucas wanted to lock the world out and never leave.

"Why do you do this to me?" Lucas buried his face in Jack's neck.

Jack laughed. "I'm not doing anything to you. You're fighting yourself, your fears and whatever you think might happen if you acknowledge this part of you. Being gay isn't the end of the world, no matter what your dad or anyone drilled into your head."

"I'm not gay," Lucas said.

"Bi or pansexual won't scare me off, but I think you know what you are. If all those girls were what you wanted, you'd never kiss me—no matter how drunk you got. You use those beautiful women to fit in and you use beer to make it easier for you to deal with them. It's really a relief to just be yourself. That's why you like me—you can be yourself and I don't judge you. I don't threaten to expose you. I'm a good guy. Newsflash, you can have that all the time. Be yourself, forget what everyone else wants and expects. You can still own a ranch and a rodeo, if that's what you love, but who you sleep with doesn't matter. People get over it. They adjust." Jack kissed Lucas' neck.

Lucas pulled away. "People buy the package. The story. It's what they want. If you change it, they feel betrayed. They'd call me a liar hiding who he really is. Celebrity gets no sympathy. They'd never understand about my father. I can't tell them how my father acted and talked about gay guys. My mother would flip out—she has her memories of him. I'm not blowing up my family—not what I have left. Let's drop this. I'll text the owner and see when we can swing by to chat and see the bull."

His hands were better off busy on the phone with something that mattered regardless of how much Lucas wanted to rip Jack's clothes off.

Every word Jack had said rang true and Lucas wanted it. He wanted to be himself and to hell with what people thought. Other than his mom and brothers, it didn't matter—well, Jack. More than anything, Lucas wanted Jack to want him. Not to act like he was just helping some random closet case, but him. Jack talked like a guy who wanted more than sex but things were too complicated even for that. Lucas was a patient. Maybe that was why Jack was keeping things at a certain distance? It hurt, but what was Lucas offering anyway?

"This sort of stuff doesn't change. It just consumes from the inside until it comes out. I'm not going to say anything, but don't play with me like I'm a toy in your closet." Jack slid a hand to the front of Lucas' jeans. "Feels real to me."

Lucas pushed himself away from Jack. "I don't have time for this."

Jack backed off as Lucas' phone rang. Lucas didn't recognize the name so he ignored it.

Calming himself down, Lucas thought of anything but Jack. The pain in his back helped. "You don't have to help me anymore. I'll find someone else for the PT or do these exercises alone."

Jack got right back into Lucas' space. "No. I'm the best. I can be professional. Believe it or not, I can keep my hands off you. Might be easier if you dealt with this. Let it happen, because running away won't solve it."

"You didn't run? You went to the military," Lucas said.

Jack sighed. "I did. My dad wanted me to be a doctor. I didn't want that. I talked to a few and I wanted to help people but not be pressured or educated into hating my job. Dad wouldn't pay for college if I wasn't pre-med. I got certified as a paramedic and the military had opportunities. My dad is a bit of a bully. I had to stand up on my own and be away from him to find myself, my voice. All that other stuff would be the same, straight or gay. If you think that's running, you might want to run there. I came back to Dallas and finished my education. I could've gone anywhere but I didn't."

"My dad was a bit of a bully too. You get along with yours now?" Lucas asked.

"He hates the tattoo, but he knows he can't change me. His money can't control me. I work hard and I take care of myself, so what can he do?" Jack asked.

"He can hate you, shame you," Lucas said.

Jack put his hands on Lucas' shoulder and Lucas tensed.

"Is that what your dad did to you?" Jack asked.

"You don't know my dad," Lucas said.

"No, but I'm sure I've dealt with men like him before. Being what he wanted you to be, are you lying to yourself? If it's not who you are, then you're only hurting you and keeping everyone else at bay. There's no award for straightest-acting gay cowboy in your rodeo." Jack let Lucas go and put the file back together.

Lucas grabbed the copies. They left with a tense silence between them.

In the truck, Lucas' phone rang again before he'd started the drive.

The number was unlisted and he hoped it was a lead on what happened to the bull.

"Hello," Lucas answered.

"Mr. Burr, I'm with the *Metroplex Daily* here in Dallas. I have just a few questions," the man rattled off quickly.

Lucas swore to himself. "I'll be back in the saddle in no time. Thanks."

Cutting off the call, Lucas then blocked the number.

"Who was that?" Jack asked.

"The press. My massive public wanting to know when I'll be back. Should I let them all down?" Lucas asked.

"If you think liking men will let them down, you don't get the sport. They pay to see you ride and fall. They won't love you less if you're married with kids, divorced or on your fourth wife," Jack pointed out.

"Gay rodeo guys take a lot more harassment," Lucas replied.

"So you're a wimp? Or you just don't want people to know and lump you in with those guys? Because I really doubt anyone would harass one of the star riders and owners of a major rodeo," Jack taunted.

Lucas gripped the steering wheel. "It could hurt business. Should I drop you back at the PT office?"

"Sure. I've got some clients later." Jack sighed. "You could make it easier on those gay cowboys, showing them they aren't alone. A little dip in sales and people will forget all about it in a month."

"My rodeo is fair. Everyone is welcome. You want to rodeo? You'd make a good gay cowboy," Lucas shot back.

Jack smiled. "No. I have no desire to injure myself on a regular basis. That's not my adrenaline fix. I enjoy helping people. Not everyone wants the spotlight. If it's what you love, great, but you can do something good with your celebrity too. Or you could quit and have a private life. Who cares as long as you're happy?"

Lucas wasn't sure what he wanted, other than Jack to shut up and get in his bed. "My mama, Greg and my brothers."

"They want you to be happy. You know you left out your dad," Jack reminded him.

Lucas took a corner too sharp. "Sorry."

Jack braced himself but slid along the seat close to Lucas.

Finally, Lucas parked outside Jack's work.

"The longer you fight it, the harder it gets. But if you want to be miserable, who am I to tell you that you can be happy? Maybe you haven't met the right guy yet." Jack hopped out and headed inside.

Lucas stared at the building as his mind spun. Letting go of the feelings, he focused on the mystery at hand. Where was that bull? Had someone messed with it or was he just using this as a way to distract himself from Jack while being closer to him?

No, something was off that day. Lucas was sure of that before he'd even met Jack. The injury was messing with his dating life and Jack was a safe outlet who wouldn't tax his back—like in prison it was his only option.

* * * *

"We are done for today," Teddy declared.

"Another peaceful day with a Burr in my saddle," Jack teased.

"Ouch. Most of the women around here just keep offering to take him off your hands," Teddy replied.

"They'd either be too easy on him or end up in a struggle. I think he just enjoys fighting a bit." Jack smiled as he headed for the break room.

Ken walked in. "Jack, got a minute?"

"Sure." He followed him to the office. "Not another rodeo clown."

"The helpers don't like to be called clowns anymore. But no, no more rodeo guys. I know Lucas is a pain, but you're hanging in there and trying all your tricks. That's why you're the best. Grab a seat." Ken locked the door behind Jack.

He frowned. "Is something wrong?"

"I want this to stay between us. I own the PT part of the business, not the nursing home side of things." Ken sat down behind his desk.

"That's not a secret," he replied.

Ken tapped his fingers on his desk. "Look, I know the nursing home business isn't easy. Lots of deaths, accidents and so on. I've been thinking about getting our own place. A location independent of the home. We'd still have a team that goes to work with the residents, we can offer a team to the hospital if they have people on vacation or on leave, do the house calls and we could have more space. More private rooms, more equipment and our own reputation."

"I like it. I don't think the nursing home is bad. It's a small town—most of the residents get family visiting weekly, if not more. They could use our space for another common room—maybe have one quieter and one for visitors and so on. But we've got so many clients that you could expand, hire on more and get a bigger space," Jack agreed.

"That means I'd need a partner. Someone willing to invest in it with me," he said with a grin.

"Me?" Jack asked.

"I'm just feeling people out. There is definitely promotion potential…we'll need someone to manage the staff. I'm not sure if anyone else would be interested. You're the best. You train the newbies with patience and confidence. You're practically the PT manager already. It'd tick some people off if I gave you that title now, but you already do the work. Don't think I don't notice. If we restructure, move, and you invested some amount of money—then we're partners and you're managing the staff would be less of an issue, I hope," he said.

"And what would you be doing?" Jack asked. The investor part made him hesitate.

"I have all the hospital and nursing home contacts. I'll manage the patient flow and business side. Expenses, receipts, insurance and all that boring stuff but that's how we get paid. Think about it, no need to answer now. Come up with questions. We're not rushing into it," he added.

"Thanks, I will. As for Lucas Burr," Jack began.

"He said he's happy with you. I'm sure however you're handling him is just fine," Ken replied. "Night, Jack."

Jack nodded. "Night."

As Jack headed for his truck, a text came through.

Lucas: *Time to visit the vet…got time?*

Jack: *Sure, pick you up in thirty?*

Lucas: *Great, I'll be at the guest house*

Jack ended the text with a thumbs-up and climbed in the truck. He was hardly the most logical choice for investigating a rodeo situation, but he wasn't going to object to spending more time with Lucas. The attraction was real and even if it came to nothing, he'd keep a better eye on his patient.

Then again, Lucas could've done this on his own. What the text really told Jack was that Lucas wanted more time with him. Jack couldn't help but want more too.

* * * *

Lucas was waiting on the porch as Jack pulled up. The cowboy hopped into the passenger seat and looked straight ahead.

"Missed me bad?" Jack teased.

"Don't start. The vet is going on vacation tomorrow, a month in the Bahamas. It's now or we wait to be sure. You don't have to go if you don't want." Lucas folded his arms.

"You didn't have to invite me along if you didn't want me to go." Jack pulled out of the huge ranch. "Where do we go?"

Lucas set his phone with directions between them. Jack followed the navigation prompts.

"Ken said you're happy with my services. Glad to hear it." Jack couldn't resist poking the cowboy a bit.

Lucas shifted. "I'm doing better. Your process is slow, but I want to regain my full strength."

"Good call. We'll add a bit more strength training for your core." Jack let the conversation lag for a bit.

"I hope your dog won't be going hungry because of this. I should've waited an hour," Lucas said.

"Relax, he's got an automatic feeder. Twice a day, on time. That way if I'm stuck late at work or somehow manage to score a date, he's not bothered. He never makes a mess in the house," Jack said.

"Impressive," Lucas replied.

Jack smiled. "I do wish I had a big yard for a big dog to run in. I walk him every day but he's a small dog I rescued. He loves to lie in the sun."

"Doggie door? That'd be good," Lucas agreed.

Jack found the vet's office and parked the truck. "That wasn't too far. Ready?"

Lucas just sat there for a moment, quiet.

"You okay?" Jack nudged Lucas' arm.

"Don't," Lucas warned.

"Don't act like I'm a predatory gay trying to change you. I touch people all the time. It's part of my job. If I was hitting on you, you'd know it. You're the only one whose crossed that line more than once." Jack took a deep breath, and Lucas' scent hit him in the gut.

Jack exited the truck and waited for Lucas. Finally, he followed and Jack locked the vehicle and enjoyed watching Lucas walk ahead.

They went inside and found the place empty but for one receptionist and the vet.

"We're closed. Just doing paperwork before he leaves on vacation," the receptionist said.

"I know. I called ahead. Lucas Burr. Just a quick question." Lucas pulled the copied pages from his pocket.

"Sure, go on back. The office is at the end of the hall," she said.

The door was open. Jack tapped on the wall.

"Oh, Lucas. So nice to see you. Come in. I'm Dr. Maddox." The old man reached for Jack's hand.

"Jack Gable," Jack replied.

"The PT guy. Medical types all know each other in a small town. I've heard very good things. Well, what can I do for you boys?" The old man adjusted his round glasses. He was eighty if he was a day and hunched a bit even when sitting.

"You signed off on the rodeo animals for the night I was hurt. I know falls happen but I have a reason to believe that something else may have contributed to the fall. I just wondered if you remember anything odd about that night. Anyone hanging around the bull who shouldn't be there or had an ax to grind?"

"There are always tons of people around. No one caught my attention, though. I got as good a look as ever and things seemed fine with the bull." Dr. Maddox looked over his notes. "Nothing starred or with any notes on it."

"How good of a look do you get?" Jack asked.

"Well, with those longhorns and intact bulls, you only look through the stalls. Too dangerous to handle them without sedation and that doesn't help the rodeo performance. You look for them not using all their feet, favoring one, or if there's any discharge from the eyes, nose or mouth. I always look them over for swelling, blood or discharge. It's not a complete physical but these animals are maintained by their owners. They won't even be let into the rodeo with a cough or anything contagious like roundworm. The animals infect one another easily." Maddox shrugged. "You think you got a lame bull?"

"I don't know what happened, but it felt wrong," Lucas replied.

Maddox nodded. "I do a sweep of the animals an hour before the event so there's time to swap one out if there is an issue."

"Thanks, Doc," Jack said.

"If you think of anything while sitting on that beach…" Lucas shook the doc's hand.

"Of course, you should try a vacation sometime. If you'll excuse me, a little more paperwork before I go home to pack."

They left and piled back into Jack's truck.

"Sorry I dragged you out for nothing," Lucas said

"Not at all. I never realized so many pieces go into making a rodeo," Jack admitted.

"Live animals are very unpredictable. It's possible the bull kicked the sides too hard and hurt himself before the ride. Or someone could've drugged him." Lucas studied Jack as he drove them back to the guest house.

"Just glad they didn't go after you directly," Jack added.

"What?" Lucas asked.

"Someone could've attacked you, drugged and beaten you or even killed you. People make big bets on the rodeo. One bet, one sure thing and whacked you on the knee like that Olympic skating chick. People do awful things for money or revenge," Jack said.

Lucas reached for Jack's hand on the seat between them. "Could've hurt my mom or someone else to get to me."

Jack squeezed Lucas' hand. "We'll figure it out. We could grab dinner on the way home?" he suggested.

"No thanks. I've got dinner waiting for me at the compound. I'd invite you but Mama gets mad if I don't let her know about company ahead of time. Southern ladies like to impress." Lucas smiled. "I'll see you tomorrow for more PT."

Jack pulled up all the way to the big compound this time and let Lucas out. The huge ranch could be called a mansion by some. It sprawled and Jack knew he was out of his element. His dad had money, but 'big quad brick home in a nice suburb of Dallas' cash. No wonder Lucas wanted to keep on rodeoing—it made him a massive income.

With a wave, Lucas headed inside. Jack waved back and peeled out into the night. Every eligible girl in town was after that bachelor. Jack might want more but he wasn't going to fool himself. He was just a side piece Lucas was playing with.

# Chapter Six

"What can I do to move faster?" Lucas asked at the next PT appointment.

Jack didn't want to rush through it, but he wouldn't drag things out just to spend time with Lucas. "The exercises we do here, same reps daily. You can do more at home but when your back starts to tighten, take a small break. No horses, no high-impact anything. No lifting anything over ten pounds. Now let's get out of here," Jack said.

"Where do you want to go?" Lucas followed him.

"You drive, I'll navigate." Jack opened the door, grabbed two bottles of water and went over to Lexi. "Going to take him on a hike. I've got my phone if anyone is looking for me."

Lexi smiled. "He's your last client of the day. Have fun."

Lucas opened the door to his pickup for Jack and Jack hopped in. "Thanks, but it's not a date."

Lucas chuckled. "My mama taught me manners. I'm not worried about how it looks." He closed the door and walked around the truck, without his cane.

Jack wasn't sure about that but he buckled up and checked out the vehicle. Top of the line inside and out, Jack wondered how many women Lucas had gotten into his ride. This was strictly business.

Lucas pulled out of the parking space. "Which way?"

Jack directed him away from the town to a grassy and tree-filled area.

"Here's good. Park anywhere. Do you have gym shoes to try instead of the boots?" he asked.

Lucas smiled. "Boots are all I wear."

"I hope they're custom-made with good arches," Jack said.

"You brought me here to talk about shoes?" Lucas asked.

Jack rolled his eyes. "Take a water and let's go for a slow hike."

Lucas took the water and Jack hopped out from the passenger side. Lucas exited as well and hit the button to lock the door. "You first," he said.

"Nope." Jack fell in step next to him on the footpath. His eyes darted to his feet then his shoulders. "Keep an eye out for snakes," Lucas said.

Jack laughed. "I grew up in Dallas. I'm a real Texan."

"I know but a city boy doesn't face as many snakes," he said.

Jack shook his head. "Plenty of them. My dad had land on the outskirts and worked in the city. He raised horses and some goats."

"Goats?" Lucas asked.

"My brother couldn't tolerate cow's milk. Dad turned it into a small dairy sort of thing. Then it got popular. Dad has a way of doing that. Turning things into a business. My brother and his family took over the horse part of the ranch and my other brother works with my dad, making fancy goat cheese and milk. Now they have llamas and alpacas and even a few ostriches." He shrugged.

"You must miss them?" he asked.

"I do but they're not that far away. What about your fam? Any siblings?" Jack asked.

"A couple brothers. My dad had a smaller ranch and I bought up around it. Built a big main house and stables. The house I grew up in is now the guest house," he said.

"Impressive but you put Burrwood on the rodeo map, as people keep telling me. I'm sorry I don't follow it. I saw some of your rides and your fall, for research, and I just cringe every time a guy gets flung off a horse or bull." Jack shuddered.

"Better than working on an oil rig," Lucas said.

"How's your pain?" he asked.

"I was just starting to enjoy this," he grumbled.

"Any pain?" Jack pressed.

"An ache but it's good. When I sit too much, it feels tense. This is the ache of movement. Progress," he said.

"Good. Slow walks on level ground are good for you. But not on concrete or really hard floors—you want some cushion." Jack picked up the pace just a tad. Part of him wanted to watch Lucas walk, but was it professional or personal? The smell and warmth of a real cowboy right next to Jack had him thinking things he shouldn't be.

And they weren't just sexual thoughts. He liked Lucas' voice. Being alone with him was calming and safe. Nature walks weren't really his thing. Jack would've hit the gym for an hour, but this was about Lucas. It was his job, but he didn't have to go to this much trouble. But they had some privacy out here and no one would see, so maybe Lucas could let down his guard. Also, a bad idea, he had to not be too casual or close to Lucas. Crossing that professional line could cost him his job, ruin his whatever it was with Lucas, and it'd hurt.

A hike was boring and safe. Jack wanted to take Lucas other places, like that little gay bar in town or a bigger one in Dallas just to see what Lucas thought of it. Maybe Pride in Dallas—would Lucas embrace it or run away? Jack felt stupid daydreaming about it. He couldn't drag Lucas out of the closet. Lucas had to make his choices.

Fate had given him Lucas for a patient, and Lucas wasn't going to change therapists—it'd make him look homophobic or intolerant. He also wanted Lucas around but if they got too close, Lucas would be outed and everything would change.

The bottom line was simple—screwing around with a patient was unethical. Jack would get fired. He had so little self-control around Lucas that he had to be careful not to fantasize about things or get his hopes up.

He needed to change the topic and focus on the time he had alone with Lucas.

"Since the bull seems to be fine as far as the vet is concerned, what are we thinking? Someone snuck in right before you rode and messed with the bull? Who would want to hurt you?" Jack asked.

Lucas sighed. "Let's see. A couple of ranch hands we had to fire last summer for stealing. There's a rival who has been jumpier around me in the last couple of months. An ex-girlfriend who I'd been off and on with for six months. Her family was pretty pissed off and I know I hurt her. Oh, and an investor who wanted to buy in on the rodeo. I refused. The guy is extreme right wing. I'm fine with Jesus but not people who want to burn gays and any woman who ever had a miscarriage. Nutjobs."

Jack grinned. "Yeah, that's not someone you want to be in business with."

Lucas could live in denial if he wanted but Jack was certain now that Lucas had repressed his homosexuality for some reason. He might like women but he wasn't torn between men and women. He was playing it safe instead of being happy. It was sad, but Jack couldn't let himself fall into that trap.

The sun lit up that red hair and Lucas couldn't stop stealing glances. Jack was more fun out of the office.

"Just the two brothers?" Lucas asked.

"And two sisters. They moved away when they got married so I don't see them as much. You?" he asked.

"Two brothers. Younger. One in the army—he'd like you—and the other is in college. He went away for college. Why did you stay in Burrwood?" he asked.

Jack turned and walked backward to look him in the eye. "My uncle needed help. His family is all women and he needed a guy to kick him in the ass. In Dallas, like any city, you can get lost in the shuffle. Here, I felt like I made a difference and people noticed. I ended up liking it here and stayed. That was five years ago."

"And you shot to the top of the PT world in Burrwood," he teased.

He shook his head. "Hardly. That took time and its less competition here. Dallas has plenty of hospitals and facilities. I worked for a huge orthopedic group with five surgeons. No one even noticed I was gone. If I wanted to go back, I'd find a job but here—there aren't as many resources."

"You stayed to help? Took pity on us small town folk." He swung his water bottle at Jack playfully.

"I never said that. Hardly pity. It feels good to be needed and help people. Getting people to trust you in a small town is tough. Having family here helped. The gay scene is way smaller. I'm not sure if that's good or bad yet." He smiled.

"No one you're interested in?" Lucas asked.

"Nah, Mark sounds nice but there didn't feel like a spark. The right guy will turn up. What about you, any favorite blonde groupie?" Jack asked.

Lucas turned. "I don't have a girlfriend. It helps with the fans if I'm single."

"Really? You want kids?" Jack asked casually.

"Why aren't you pushing me on the gay thing?" Lucas asked. They were out in the middle of nowhere. They could talk here.

"You want me to push you?" Jack asked.

Lucas moved into Jack's space. Both hot and sweaty from the walk, it felt right. He brushed his lips over Jack's. Jack returned the kiss but as Lucas deepened it and pulled Jack in, he felt the tension. Sliding a hand under Jack's shirt, Lucas bit his lower lip. "No one can see or hear us out here."

Jack shoved Lucas back. "Do you think I brought you here for privacy? Our own personal Brokeback? We're here for your back, not a hookup."

"But." Lucas shook his head. "I don't get it. We can."

"You want me here? I'm not your secret. I'm not ashamed. That's all on you," Jack said.

"I know but I'm not. Not really. Like you said, a hookup." Lucas couldn't stop the dreams or the desire. "You're like a drug."

"No, you're gay or bi. You want to hide and be depressed, go ahead, but you won't drag me down with you." Jack shook his head. "Now let's talk about something else. Something safe."

He sighed. "I don't want to end up like my dad."

"What happened to him?" Jack asked.

Lucas steeled himself. "Took a hoof to the sternum after a fall. Killed him instantly. I have to ride and I have to keep my family safe. I don't get to play house with a guy."

"What does one have to do with the other? You take good care of your mom. I've only seen the outside of the compound but it's huge. You ranch and rodeo. Not putting all your eggs in one basket is also smart," Jack said.

"My dad mocked guys like…like those gay cowboys that rodeo. Thought they should stick to the gay bars. Village People. And that was the nicer things than he said." Lucas shook his head.

"I'm sorry. You don't want to be like your dad. Don't hate yourself. That's a miserable life," Jack said.

"I don't hate myself. If I'm bi, it's only because my dad was such a jerk that I felt sorry for gays. I wondered why or how anyone could choose that. I know, it's not a choice but his voice still runs in the back of my head like a tape. I can't erase it," Lucas said.

Jack put his hand on Lucas' back. "You can. He's not in charge anymore. I hope you find the right woman for you. Or a guy you're worth letting yourself be happy with. Maybe Mark?"

Lucas laughed. "Definitely not Mark. He's a good guy but no chemistry. I just always come back to my ranch. The horses, the family and not screwing up."

"No one is telling you to give up horses. Your back is damaged. The weakness will be there—once injured, you can come back, but reinjury will be much easier. I'd be lying to you if I said anything else." Jack paused and looked him in the eye.

"I appreciate the honesty, but it's my life. It's what I do. I need to rodeo again," he admitted. Lucas never thought about his career ending, not until he was at least forty. That was ten more years of rodeo and celebrity. But was it enough? Could he keep up the act that long? When he thought about it, that was exhausting. A private life of ranching and running the rodeo behind the scenes sounded like heaven.

But a bit lonely. Could he have a real happy relationship? Jack seemed to think he could have a happy gay marriage and make a family in a small town in Texas. All the things Lucas' father had said was sick and wrong now felt possible—more than possible. They felt right.

Maybe the injury was really an opportunity? He could bow out of the rodeo, change his life and stop living up to what other people wanted from him. Just out himself and see how it all shook out. Now, with Jack around, it felt almost possible.

"Then mentally prep yourself for the possibility that one of those rides might end in your death or permanent paralysis. Riding a nice tame horse? That risk would be acceptable to me. Rodeo, no. You can be the face, ride and even teach the next generation of guys but you're taking a real risk with your life to ride bulls again. I couldn't live with it. That's not enough?" Jack asked.

"If I had a kid or something to think about, maybe. You never think your last ride will be your last," he replied.

Jack nodded. "You could focus on adopting a kid or something. Sorry, bad joke. Skill is great but luck plays a part. Your luck will run out one day. One day you might have a kid you want to ride a nice tame horse with, but you won't be able to."

"I do have another business to fall back on," Lucas reminded him. Lucas wasn't a one-trick pony, but the approval and admiration of people felt good. Women wanting him helped cover a lot of issues for him, but Lucas needed to remind himself that his father was dead. While the memory of Dad's commentary ran in Lucas' head like he was right there always, Lucas knew the biggest obstacle was out of the way. He felt guilty for the relief it gave him, but now Lucas was in control. He just had to stop the tape in his head.

"Good. Just don't leave it for your brothers to pick up the pieces when you die in the ring. Know when to step back from riding and be a rancher who owns part of a rodeo," Jack said.

Lucas looked him in the eye. He grabbed Jack's arm.

"What's wrong now?" Jack asked.

"Using my family to guilt me into not riding. Why?" Lucas asked.

"I'm sorry, but my job, my instinct is to keep people safe. It's your life, but I don't generally make out with my patients. I care about you and I don't want to see you in pain. I don't want you in a wheelchair. Even if I can't have you, I want you whole and happy." Jack pulled away.

Lucas caught Jack and leaned forward. They were so close. "I care too."

"Really? Seems like you want to use me for some gay-sex experiment. Take the edge off the desire so you can fake it with the blonde groupies. I'm not interested in that." Jack tried to walk away.

Lucas caught him and kissed him hard. It wasn't teasing or playful—he let his emotional wall down and the pain faded to need as he turned the kiss tender.

"Lucas, you don't need to be out to me. You need to be free in front of everyone in your life. That's what makes the pain go away. Not sex or love. Honesty. It's not an ultimatum or a game. You need to be clear on who you are and what you want." Jack kissed him softly then nuzzled his neck. "Not that the other stuff isn't great. But I can't watch you suffer struggling with it. That hurts me and then I'd try to help and you'd get frustrated. And if you're around me too much, people will talk or suspect. Then you'll blame me for outing you by association. More than anything, I don't want to hurt you."

The walk went on in a strained silence.

# Chapter Seven

That kiss had haunted Jack's dreams, daydreams and every spare second when he should have been thinking about something else. As he drove to his aunt and uncle's for Sunday dinner, he found himself wondering, *Why not have fun?*

"No! He's a patient. I could lose my job. Just when I'm up for a promotion," Jack lectured himself. He'd found patients attractive before but usually they had a wife or girlfriend and it was easy for Jack to write them off as unavailable.

Hooking up without feelings…he could do it, but he already had some feelings about Lucas. "He's getting back in the rodeo. I'd just be worried all the time that he'd end up dead or paralyzed. That's too much. It's crazy," Jack told himself as he pulled into the driveway.

He took a moment to calm down. Then Dot tapped on the driver's window.

Jack jumped and put the window down. "Hi. Sorry, I was thinking."

"Lost in those thoughts. Come inside and share. It's easier to solve a problem with lots of brains on it," Dot said.

Jack nodded but his phone rang. "It's a patient. Let me get this," Jack replied. He put up the window and took the call. Lucas had the worst timing.

"Hello," Jack said.

"Hey, how are you?" Lucas asked.

Jack frowned at the phone. "Fine. I'm on my way to my aunt's for dinner. Can I help you with something?"

"Sorry, I didn't know. I managed to track down one of the ranch hands that we let go last year," Lucas explained.

"And?" Jack prompted.

"The guy was picked up by ICE a few months back, so it couldn't be him. I'd say a friend or family member might be out for revenge on me, but with ICE involved, they have bigger problems than a ranch hand job." Lucas sighed.

Jack stifled a laugh. "Well it's probably not him. One guy off your suspect list. Good."

"What? What's funny about that?" Lucas asked.

"Really? You said *ranch hand job*. I've never had one of those. Maybe you're not gay," Jack replied.

Lucas snickered. "Poor choice of words. You don't have to make everything about sex."

"I'm not the one making all the moves and then hiding. It was a joke. I'm not playing games. One suspect down, great. we need to talk to the bull's owner and see if the bull was off or injured post ride, but I have to go into dinner. Talk tomorrow?" Jack asked.

"Sure, sorry. I didn't mean to interrupt." Lucas hung up.

Jack sighed and stared at his phone. Never in his life had he ever wanted a guy so much and at the same time wanted to distance himself so they didn't get hurt.

* * * *

Sitting on the porch, Lucas had to distract himself from Jack. Trying to find out who'd sabotaged him was good, but he couldn't do much on a Sunday afternoon. He walked over to the stables and his favorite horse came out to greet him.

The animal shifted like he wanted to go out for a ride.

"You always want to get me in trouble." Lucas patted the horse on the side.

He looked at the calm, steady beast. He wasn't saddled, but Lucas led him over to the raised porch where he could climb on without stressing his back. *Just swing my leg over.*

Grabbing the reins, Lucas willed himself on. Fire erupted in his lower back but he gripped with his legs. The posture was natural and he thought getting back to it would feel better, it would make him stronger. This horse wouldn't throw him—it wasn't rodeo. The searing pain disagreed with his logic. He leaned forward for support.

"What are you doing, *jefe*?" asked one of the ranch hands.

"I just really need to be back in the saddle for a minute, Enrique," Lucas said.

Enrique shook his head. "I don't see a saddle, boss. You might want to get down. I think you took too many pain meds."

"I didn't take any," Lucas corrected.

"Then it might be worse." Enrique turned. "Jay, Tiny—give me a hand here."

The two other hands came out from the barn. One had a rope. Tiny, who was the complete opposite of his nickname, marched up.

Jay and Enrique roped and held the horse.

"Climb off, boss." Tiny turned his back.

"I'm fine," Lucas insisted.

"Boss lady will be mad if she sees this," Enrique warned.

"My mother isn't the boss of me," Lucas replied.

"Pissing off any woman is a bad idea, no matter who the real boss is," Jay added.

Tiny shrugged. "Arms around my neck and I gently pull you off, boss. You slid down, your feet hit the ground and we're good."

It was a solid plan, but Lucas hated that he'd failed. "He's a gentle horse."

"You look like you're in pain," Jay said.

Lucas grabbed Tiny around the neck. "Pull."

Seconds later, Lucas' boots touched solid earth and he let go of Tiny.

His back betrayed him and he doubled over.

"Okay, we gotcha," Jay said.

"I'll put the horse away, you get him inside. Take something for the pain," Enrique advised.

Lucas nodded. "I'm sure you're right."

Jay and Tiny got on solid ground. Lucas grabbed an ice pack and slid it down his lower back then took some ibuprofen. He went for his truck, feeling better than he had a week ago.

* * * *

Lucas found himself at the bar again. Sunday night was a bad time to be out drinking but he had limited himself to one alcoholic drink. He couldn't get Jack out of his head.

"Jack's not here today," Mark said as he poured Lucas a cup of coffee.

"I know. I just needed to get away from my thoughts. I'm not looking for anyone," Lucas said.

"Okay. If you run into Jack, put in a good word for me. Hard to find guys like that," Mark said.

"In this bar, yeah. Why not work at the other one?" Lucas asked.

Mark grinned. "Ladies tip well here if I flirt. Not as much patronage at the other bar except on certain party nights. Plus, it gives me a place to go that isn't work and is fun. Boundaries are good."

"Makes sense." Lucas studied the bartender as he waited on another patron.

Mark was good-looking in tight jeans and a tighter T-shirt. Boots and a big belt buckle—but no spark. Spark was essential. Jack and Lucas had that spark so deeply and instantly that Lucas felt like an idiot. He could admire men for their looks but when they opened their mouth, he wanted to get away from them. With Jack, Lucas wanted more…more conversation, more kissing, more hikes and more of everything. Dinners and chores—Jack would make everything better. With Jack, he didn't feel alone…he felt whole.

Alvin and Pete slid onto the stools next to Lucas. "Hey," Lucas said.

"Hey, best rodeo rider not riding," Pete joked.

Pete was a useless hanger-on of Alvin's. Alvin, however, was the rival who'd been a jerk to Lucas lately. Lucas couldn't complain when the suspects came to him.

"Next one is on me," Alvin said.

"I've had my limit of drinks, thanks," Lucas said.

Al and Pete shared a look. Pete grabbed Lucas' drink and sniffed. "Coffee? You want to at least make it Irish?"

"I don't need more with the meds I'm on." Lucas wasn't taking the pain meds, but it was good enough of an excuse for these jerks.

"Come on. One shot. Take one for your recovery," Pete joked.

"Maybe that little gay army PT boy has whipped Lucas into shape?" Alvin teased.

Lucas shook his head. "You know, you and I used to be okay and lately it's weird. I don't know if you wanted to take me out or just see me get hurt but I knew someone messed with that bull."

"What?" Al snorted and choked on his shot. "You think I sabotaged you?"

"He ain't that much of a planner," Pete said.

Al nodded. "For sure. Pete, go take a leak."

"I don't have to go," Pete said.

"Go," Al said.

Pete went off, mumbling.

Al shook his head. "I didn't try to hurt you, man. I've been different, yeah. But I'm not out to hurt another rider. I'm dating Cathy. We kept it quiet because she didn't want to upset you. I thought maybe you found out or something. I've just been keeping my distance. I'm not into hurting anyone or cheating."

"Why did you want Pete to leave?" Lucas asked.

Al shrugged. "He'd want Cathy to set him up with someone. She's a good woman. I don't know why you let her go, but I'm not stupid."

"You're right. She's a great woman. Just not the right spark, you know? She's attractive and we gave it a go, but I didn't want to waste her time. You treat her right or you'll answer to me," Lucas said.

"Not a problem. I'm sparking with her plenty and treating her like an angel. Not that I'd admit to being whipped to anyone but her ex… Sure I can't get you a beer?" Al offered.

"Nah, I'm good. I should go home and get some rest for the PT torture tomorrow. By the way." Lucas grabbed Al by his bolo tie. "Don't talk trash about Jack. He's the best at what he does. I only work with the best. Got it?"

Al gasped and nodded. "Got it."

"Good." Lucas smacked Al on the back.

He tossed money down to cover his tab and left.

Another suspect eliminated. Lucas was sure Al didn't go to the trouble—he'd been squirrely because of Cathy. But Lucas had to watch how he reacted if people took shots at Jack. Defending a friend was one thing, but he couldn't overreact again or Mark might suspect something.

# Chapter Eight

A ringing phone at one in the morning was worse than the alarm on a Monday.

Jack's heart pounded, and he prayed it wasn't an accident or a health issue with a family member. He'd left his aunt and uncle fine, but things changed quickly.

Rubbing his eyes, he leaned over and looked at the phone. The screen said Lucas. "Butt dial or drunk dial?" he muttered to himself.

When the ringing didn't stop, he grabbed the phone off his nightstand and answered. "Hello?"

"Um, Jack? Is that you?" Lucas asked.

"Yeah, what's wrong? Did you fall?" he asked.

Normally physical therapist didn't get the late-night calls. Patients called their doctor, got the answering service and were patched through to the doc or told to call 911. The smart ones just called 911 because a fall meant going to get X-rays and scans to be sure there was no new damage. Calling the physical therapist was just weird, but Lucas might well be drunk.

"No, I had a few drinks with some friends. I crashed at the guest house, I guess. But I had a dream. This is stupid, I'm sorry." Lucas sighed.

Jack sat up in bed. Plenty of patients had a freak-out about their recovery, but normally they did it in the PT room. "It's okay. Just tell me what it was about."

"No, I'm not—I'm fine," he said.

"You're not fine. You can trust me," Jack said.

"I need you to come here. I can't do this on the phone," Lucas said.

He frowned. "Fine. I'll be there in half an hour. Just have some coffee or toast or something."

Jack ended the call and pulled on jeans and a T-shirt. After quick trip to the bathroom to freshen up, he grabbed his keys. Roscoe, the chihuahua, barked at the disturbance, turned around and went back to sleep in his little dog bed. At the front door of his apartment, Jack shoved his feet in gym shoes and was ready.

"Shhh, I'll be back," Jack reassured his dog.

Coffee would've been a good idea, but he wanted to get there fast and make sure Lucas hadn't hurt himself. Maybe he'd fallen out of bed or in the shower—something that was embarrassing. The thought of him naked woke Jack up, but he hadn't heard any water so that was very unlikely.

Clients had done weirder things. Sex before they should could lead to serious injury. If Lucas had been out drinking with friends, maybe he'd taken a lady home and wrenched his back trying to prove that he could be everything he'd been before the fall.

Jack pulled into the long drive of the ranch. The sprawling main house with wraparound porch had flood lights and was easy to spot at the end of the drive. Beyond that, barns were visible. About halfway up the drive, off to the left, was another house that looked like an average home.

He turned and parked in front of it, next to Lucas' truck. Jack walked up to the front door and knocked.

"Come in," Lucas said.

He walked in to the view of Lucas' tall body sprawled on the blue and white plaid sofa. One boot was on the back of the sofa, the other propped on a solid oak coffee table.

"At least your back is supported," Jack said.

Lucas grinned. "All business. Tell me I'll ride again."

"What's wrong? What did you dream about?" Jack sat on the other end of the sofa.

He struggled to sit up and Jack moved to help him. The warmth of his body and scent of leather on a man made Jack want to move closer. But the waft of beer on his breath wasn't as pleasant.

"Want some coffee?" he asked.

Lucas shook his head. "This place isn't stocked unless someone is staying here. I had a dream that I tried to ride but I couldn't. It was like I was being stabbed in the back. I had to be carried off the horse to the hospital. I couldn't move my legs."

"Okay, after your actual fall you couldn't move your legs because of the swelling. Are you sure it's not just a bad memory?" he asked.

Lucas shook his head. "This was in front of a lot of people—my comeback ride. They said I should be able to ride and I failed. I couldn't even climb the fence."

Jack stood and headed for the country-style kitchen. He poked around the cabinets with carved hearts in the oak wood. It was a charming house. In the back of one cabinet, he found a tin box of herbal tea.

There were mugs on a rack along the counter. He filled a mug with water and microwaved it. Making him tea, Jack hoped it'd help soothe Lucas or snap him out of the beer fog.

He walked over. "Here, sip this."

"Whiskey would be better," he said.

"You'd be better off not drinking. It's not a good way to manage your pain. Pain meds would help," Jack said.

"People get hooked on that crap," Lucas said.

"But not alcohol?" he teased.

"Fair enough. I know I can stop drinking any time. I don't want to complicate things," Lucas said.

"But medication doesn't make you drunk. You could've fallen and hurt your back. The wrong activity could cause a setback," Jack said.

"Activity?" Lucas smirked at Jack. "We'll just keep going in circles on the alcohol versus pills debate."

Jack grabbed a decorative pillow and smacked Lucas' shoulder. "Too much dancing, running or sexual activity and you could irritate your injury. That'll slow your recovery."

Lucas shook his head. "I didn't do any of those things. The dream wasn't just about my attempt to ride. It went in a different direction. So much worse."

Jack stroked Lucas' hair. "Talk me through it."

Slowly, he shifted from sitting next to him to lying with his head in Jack's lap. His whole body warmed to Lucas. Jack massaged Lucas' neck and worked his hand down Lucas' shoulder and back…walking various lines but he couldn't get enough.

"I tried to get on a horse. I was sitting with people and they brought out a horse. Someone said I was ready. I didn't see you but I thought I was ready. So did everyone around me," he said.

"And?" Jack slid his hand back to Lucas' neck and gently worked out a knot or two.

"I couldn't stand. I couldn't move my legs at all. Then it all changed. I was on the porch in a wheelchair. I couldn't feel my legs or move them at all. My life was over," he said.

"It was just a dream," Jack said.

"It felt so real." He wrapped his arms around Jack's waist.

Jack reached over. Instead of the pat on the back Lucas expected, Jack pinched his thigh.

"Ow," he said.

"Good, you're not paralyzed. You can feel below the waist. It was just a dream. Mixed with a drink or two, it felt real. Your body doesn't react as sharply when you're drinking. I get what you're feeling, but don't make this trigger some overcorrection. Don't work out too much or back off. Don't drink more," Jack warned.

"I won't. I needed to know I'm not crazy," he said.

"You're not crazy. You had a weird dream. Look, you'll be able to ride normal horses with no problem. I promise. When I'm done with you, you'll be fine to ride a horse, drive a car or motorcycle, line dance and have all the sex you want. But your back, the injuries to the discs—that won't vanish. Those areas will always be more susceptible to injury than the areas of your spine that weren't damaged. The pain will start there," he explained.

Panic started to creep up. "I could end up paralyzed?"

"Any one of us could. One car accident and you don't want to know what could happen to your life. I work with kids who were after a sports scholarship and one fall or one crash and it's over. Does that mean I tell people not to drive?" he asked.

"No," he answered.

"No, that's crazy. I don't tell kids not to play sports either. We all take risks in our lives every day. Some people like extreme sports and that's where it gets dicey with injuries. If you're an adrenaline junkie, it's hard."

"Don't rodeo," he groaned.

"I'm not your mother. But if you keep on with the rodeo, your odds of paralysis or major spine damage are triple that of someone who rides tame horses and ranches for a living." Jack rubbed his back.

Lucas felt like a kid but his body wasn't reacting to Jack's attention like a kid. "The rodeo isn't worth as much if I'm not riding."

"That's a big ego. You really believe they won't find another star?" Jack teased.

"I'm already a star—it's easier to keep using me," he replied.

Jack stroked his hair again. "Using you. Is that how it feels?"

"Sometimes." He yawned. "I suck at barrel racing."

The truth was it felt good to be needed, but that had crossed over to being used years ago. His dad had used him as an excuse to travel the rodeo circuit, cheat on his mom and make a lot of money betting on the side. Lucas had loved riding and the attention but he'd also known that if his younger brothers were good at it, they'd be along too. It hadn't been about love or time with Dad. It had been about earning. That had never bothered Lucas—he'd wanted to help his mom and family. The ranch hadn't brought in enough then, especially when Dad had liked expanding the land without utilizing it well enough to pay for the additions.

But this was different, in a way. He owned a quarter of the rodeo. He was using himself—keeping the fans happy meant tickets sold and butts in seats. Ranching could have bad years for prices or for harvest. All the eggs in one basket wasn't smart. Raising chickens along with cattle and horses was a good move.

Greg was part of the problem, rolling over Lucas with his promo ideas all the time and not hitting the brakes. Part of Lucas felt sorry for Greg. His prime was over and he was alone. He needed more clients, not to just focus on Lucas. The pressure—the expectation all on Lucas was too much. But when people depended on him, he didn't want to not deliver. If he had a family of his own, he'd have to provide for them.

"You could just mentor younger riders. Be a part owner in all of it. Men don't rodeo forever. There's a limit to what you can put your body through. Pick a successor."

He laughed. "Put myself out to pasture."

"No, step back and run things instead of risking your neck. Help with the kids' program or train younger men. You can still ride a horse. But you need to listen to your body and not go for broke because a crowd wants you to," Jack said.

"Washed up at thirty."

"No, not washed up. If you want a pity party, you called the wrong person. I get that you have fears about your recovery, but humans get sick, bones break, and it's not just you. You got lucky." Jack poked his shoulder.

"I know," he mumbled.

"No, you don't. You could've landed on your neck or head and be dead." Jack nudged him.

Lucas sat up and looked at Jack. So casual and handsome as the devil, the guy next door had a fire inside him. "We have a fund that helps riders who are permanently injured. A couple guys did end up in wheelchairs. I don't bitch around them."

"Don't bitch around anyone. I learned that quick in this job. Even with my colleagues. If you want to be a leader, if you want to be the best, you can't complain. Do the crap jobs without complaining, and people like you more. Then you get better chances. People like you. That's why they want you back on the bull. They like to interview you because you have a positive energy," Jack said.

Lucas smiled. "I guess. You're the only person I really bitch to like this. It feels safe."

"You ride well but a million guys can ride and get tossed," he said.

"Sure, the wannabes are endless," he said.

"You love it. That shows. You won't love the rodeo world or ranch life less if you can't ride the bulls and broncs. I'm sure the business side keeps you busy. Once you have a family, they won't want you risking your neck anyway. Most rodeo guys are probably done by thirty. Most athletes are done by then. Forty at the latest. It's not a failure, your body isn't at its peak condition anymore," he said.

"I'd like to prove you wrong there," Lucas teased.

Jack smiled. "For bull riding, you never will. Ranching, riding tame horses, having a family and a great business—those you're in your prime for right now. Or you will be when I'm done with you."

Lucas got the message. It was similar to the one his mom had given him. They didn't want him to get his hopes up. He had to ride again. He had to prove himself. "Thanks, but crowds love a comeback."

"Just don't rush it." Jack nodded. "Why are you here if you live at the main house?"

"My mom doesn't like it that I drink. She really doesn't like it if I bring ladies home. All that happens here. I like the idea of a big family ranch, but everyone knows your business. I needed some privacy." He frowned.

Jack smiled. "If you're married, you don't have to worry about it. I'm sure she'd love to have grandkids."

"She would. She'd be a great grandma. But how do you know someone is right?" he asked.

"I'm a physical therapist, not a matchmaker or dating coach. And I'm single so I don't know how to find the right one," he admitted.

"Mark asked about you," Lucas teased.

Jack rolled his eyes. "I work a lot and most of my patients are older or married. No spark Mark—I don't know. I always like the guys who say they're straight."

"Some guy in the army?" Lucas asked.

"How'd you guess? We had to sneak around back then but stateside, he went back to women. Claimed it was fun. He just wanted something different while deployed and it wasn't real. People use each other sometimes," Jack said.

"That sucks. I'm sorry." Lucas looked Jack in the eye. He didn't want to hurt Jack either. "I meet a lot of fans or girls in bars. It's not real."

"They want the rodeo star, not the man," Jack said. "Another reason to plan when you step back from riding. People will see you as a successful businessman, not just a rider."

"Hmm, you and my mom are in cahoots," he teased.

"Cahoots? I've lived in Texas all my life and that's the first time I've been accused of being in cahoots. You're such a cowboy." Jack stood up. "And you're fine. I'll see you in the morning for PT."

"Wait." Lucas pulled out his phone and checked the time. "Damn, I need more sleep. Can we meet in the afternoon?"

"I have other clients," he said.

"You can't rearrange?" he asked. He was supposed to be the priority. "Hang on. I have a message from the bull owner. That bull is out of town right now. He said no one reported injury or an odd behavior. He'll let me know when the bull is back in town."

"That's something," Jack said.

"And I ran into my rival at the bar. I don't think he did it. Maybe I'm just paranoid," Lucas said.

Jack folded his arms. "You've still got a list of suspects to work through. I'll move your PT to the afternoon and we can hit the next suspect on your list. You need more sleep and I'm feeling like a zombie."

"Yes, mom, I mean sir." He grinned.

Jack leaned down, pressing his body to Lucas. The heat and raw hard masculine feel made Lucas gasp. "What?"

"I'm a man. If you want me to punch you to prove it, I will. If you want me to screw your brains out, I can do that too," Jack promised.

Lucas tried to sit up and he only ground against Jack more. "Sorry, I didn't mean it like that."

Jack glared at Lucas dead in the eye. "Yes, you did. If you've been playing with me, thinking I won't judge you and you're not ready for women yet—I don't appreciate it. Maybe I was wrong. Maybe you're not a closet case—maybe you're just a user.

"All that kissing, flirting and now calling me in the middle of the night. This happens with medical care professionals. Patients get dependent on them and think it's more than it is. You're my job, not my life or my family," Jack said.

"I'm not using you. You kick my ass more than coddle me," Lucas argued.

Jack smiled. "Because that's what you need. Your fam and Greg baby you."

"You're the one who volunteered to investigate with me. Isn't that a line crossed?" Lucas asked.

"You want me to stop? Fine, I will. When we're done with your therapy, you can figure yourself out. I'm done playing your game," Jack said.

When he tried to get up, Lucas grabbed Jack around the waist.

"I don't know how to fix this, but I might never have met you if I didn't have this injury. You're the third guy I've kissed in my life so it's… I'm sorry if you think I'm using you but I'm not. That army guy was a jerk, but you deserve better," Lucas said.

Jack leaned in a bit closer. "You're better?"

Lucas shook his head. "I want to be. Damn sparks."

Lucas rolled Jack into a kiss. Returning the kiss, Jack grabbed Lucas' ass and pulled him in tight. "You're hard," Jack said.

"So are you. Don't stop." Lucas pressed for more heat through the layers of clothing. He ground against Jack's body.

Jack moved up Lucas' body and opened his fly.

"What?" Lucas pulled away. "What if someone comes in?"

Jack zipped and buttoned up his jeans. "You said you bring women here. We're two adults."

"You seriously think it's no big deal? My reputation." Lucas sat up on the couch.

"Your reputation? You're ashamed. You're selfish. See you at one for your appointment." Jack walked out and slammed the door behind him.

# Chapter Nine

Lucas woke to a ringing phone. It was Greg so he ignored it in favor of slipping back to the main house for a shower and a shave.

The old tricks weren't working. When he needed to feel better, drinks with friends and pretty girls usually did wonders. Last night he'd called his physical therapist to help? He felt stupid and embarrassed. Jack was all Lucas had dreamed about even after Jack had left.

On one hand it worked, calming him down about his weird dreams and fears. Jack had cut through the crap for Lucas but things had almost crossed a line. He didn't want to lose Jack as a friend and sex would definitely make a mess of things. Jack was right. Lucas had been taught to be ashamed—Dad had hammered in those opinions. It'd never felt selfish until Jack. Before, it had usually been other guys who equally wanted to keep their private stuff private. No one got hurt, no one dared to want more. Now it stung from the reality that he did want more.

In fresh clothes, Lucas felt better. He checked his phone as he walked out into the kitchen.

"Morning, sunshine. You look rough." Mama had her purse and rodeo jacket on.

"I'm okay. Didn't sleep great." He poured a cup of coffee. "Where are you off to?"

"Some of the rodeo ladies are doing a quilting circle and making things for a charity fair. I'm not quite sure what they're raising money for but I was asked to drop in and help. Then the rodeo kids are this afternoon," she said.

He smiled. "Have fun."

"Don't you have PT this morning?" she asked.

"It got moved to this afternoon. I'm going. No need to fuss," he said.

"There's a plate of eggs and bacon in the microwave if you're hungry. You need more than just toast and coffee. Greg has been calling for you all morning," she said.

"Get rid of the landline, Ma," he said.

"You pay the bills. We moved it all in your name. I was just fine in the guest house." She left through the back door.

That was a big lie, but she believed it. The cleaning lady came twice a week and he'd just have hired a housekeeper if it wouldn't insult his mother's southern cooking and homemaking sensibilities. She liked being the matriarch of a big ranch home like on one of her old soap favs, *Dallas* or *Dynasty*.

He warmed up the food and ate the eggs while sharing the bacon with Baby, the dog had a nose for people food. Finally, he gave in and called Greg.

"Where have you been all morning?" Greg asked.

"Didn't sleep great," he said.

"Does that mean a woman?" Greg asked.

"No. It means I drank a bit and had a bad night. Bad dreams," he said.

"I'll get you a nightlight and a teddy bear. We need to get your name out there with the right image," Greg said.

"I'm doing the PT program. No more pushing, no more cutting corners," Lucas answered.

"That's good for your back, not for business. We need to update people. I've had a lot of interest. A magazine wants to do a photo shoot with you on a bull, and a mini interview. They want to cover your inspiring recovery story. The publicity can't hurt," Greg said.

"What magazine? Is this online?" he asked.

"Does it matter? I thought it might help your ego too. People love a comeback story and we need them to root for you," Greg reminded him.

"It's only been a month…or, well, I guess nearly two now. I haven't been out that long," he argued.

"It doesn't take long for people to move on. You and I both have seen it. Some guy goes off with a girl for a summer instead of riding and when he comes back, we've filled his spots. He's not a name anymore. He has to re-earn it," Greg said.

"I'm an owner—no one takes my spot. Plus this is an injury not a fling," Lucas insisted.

Greg sighed. "Sure, we know that but this helps keep your public informed. It keeps your name out there. It's a few pictures and a quick interview. People don't have the attention span they used to. It won't be a deep dive into a long article. Another bonus for rodeo—quick rides."

"I always wonder if they're rooting for us to stay on or fall," Lucas said.

"They're cheering for you. That's all that matters. You're going to fall off. We all know it. But an injury and a comeback—that can be spun for good. Will you do it?" Greg asked.

"Let me think about it. I've got PT this afternoon. I'll let you know later," Lucas replied.

"Maybe we can have them get some pics of that. Good to see it's working," Greg added.

"We'll talk later. Bye." Lucas ended the call.

He wanted to run it by Jack but didn't want Greg to get the wrong idea. No one was suspecting anything, but Lucas felt like everyone knew just by glancing at him. He just needed to talk to Jack and smooth things over—he needed Jack in his corner, if no one else.

But he also needed to sort out another suspect on his list. He scrolled through his contacts and hit Cathy's number.

"Are you drunk?" Cathy answered the phone.

"No, I just wanted to talk. See how you are," he said.

"I'm doing great. How's the back?" she asked.

"You heard about that?" He chuckled.

"I'm sure all of Burrwood did. If you're looking for pity sex, I've got a new man. I'm not screwing it up," she said.

"I heard. Alvin. No, it's not about that. I just thought maybe we could grab dinner and talk about a few things. I need to apologize and I wanted to pick your brain about something," he said.

"My brain? You were never interested in my brain," she shot back.

He sighed. "I'm trying to make it up to you. Apologize."

"You think my boyfriend will like me going to dinner with an ex?" she asked.

"No, but don't worry. I won't come alone. We'll be chaperoned, if that's what you're worried about. Bring your aunt or your sister if you want," he offered.

"Those gossips. You don't want that. Fine, I'll pick an expensive restaurant and text you the reservation time," she replied.

"Sounds good, thanks," he said.

She ended the call. Lucas smiled. He didn't want to spook her by talking about sabotage of the bull. That could all wait for a face-to-face chat. With knowing she was with Alvin, odds were it wasn't Cathy. However, she had probably been at the rodeo that night since Alvin was, so he had to rule her out.

* * * *

Lucas had been distracted all session. He did the work but seemed lost in thought. Jack felt like he'd made a big mistake going to see him last night.

"Look, we can just forget about last night. The move. You made it all clear," Jack said.

"Sure. Great. I want us to be friends, okay?" Lucas asked.

"'I'm not sure we can do that. I'm your physical therapist and once your treatment plan is over, we'll see," he said.

"Fair enough. I did set up dinner with my ex to see if she knows anything about my accident. But she's dating that rival of mine," Lucas said.

Jack nodded. "The rival you think is innocent. Okay."

"Right, but she might know something else. She's always been a rodeo groupie. I want to make sure Al is treating her right too. I don't trust some of these rodeo guys. They can be players," Lucas replied.

"So I've seen. Maybe I should ask out Mark," Jack replied. "Don't worry. I'll get you out of here in time for your dinner."

"You're coming too," Lucas said.

"Why? You don't want people to get the wrong idea," Jack taunted.

Lucas sighed. "I know. But that's how Cathy feels. If she and I go out alone, Al might be out to fight me. You're the buffer."

"Me?" Jack shook his head. "The gay friend?"

"She's an ex and a friend who is concerned about my recovery. You're coming along to talk about my recovery. That's all," Lucas explained.

"This is some high school crap," Jack warned.

"You're helping me investigate this, right?" Lucas asked.

"Fine, I agreed so I will. But you're paying," Jack said.

"Agreed all around," Lucas laughed. "But I do need to pick your brain now. Do you think I could sit on a horse or bull for a while? Not riding but just sitting for a photo shoot," he explained.

"Photo shoot? Are you getting pressure to get back to work?" Jack asked.

"Plenty but this is just publicity. Talking about my recovery. They want a bull." He shrugged.

Jack shook his head. "You know bulls better than I do. I can't imagine it'll stay still."

He smiled. "They'd probably partially sedate it."

"That doesn't seem very good for the animal. I mean, if it needed medical attention or something. But just for pictures. Sorry, this is none of my business. That's your business and I'm not an expert." He sighed. "Can you sit like that for a bit? Yes. It will put more pressure on your lower back so it will ache and I'd take breaks if it's going to be longer than a few minutes."

"You can say no. I can blame you," Lucas teased.

Jack put the PT tools away. "I know a lot of people are counting on you. Your business isn't just for you and paying your bills. With the unpredictability of a wild animal, I'd say no. But you have to do what's best for you. Your health and safety are my only priority. The rodeo won't end because one rider takes a break to recover. It's your life and there are more considerations, but I'd recommend putting it off if possible."

"Fame is fleeting," Lucas reminded Jack.

"If fame is what you want, then that photo shoot sounds like it'll keep your reputation alive. Create a buzz or whatever they want to do. Just remember it's not the only way. You can make another choice and protect jobs and people as well as yourself." Jack patted Lucas' shoulder.

"Everyone likes to be cheered and applauded," he said.

"True, but what means more? A crowd of strangers or your family? I've seen people recover because their family cheers them on and needs them, not strangers," Jack replied.

"When you're the strong one, no one thinks you need the attention. The cheers and applause are nice, but it's what they really represent. Tickets sold, people entertained—getting what they paid for. Seeing someone who grew up just where they did be good at something. I'm selling a dream," Lucas said.

"People will still dream those dreams if you don't ride anymore. If you're just the MC or the owner. You're putting too much pressure all on you. It's a night of entertainment for most of the crowd. Everyone's dreams are different."

"We have an announcer. I don't want to go rounds with you on this. My mama is just as bad. She wants me safe, but she loves the rodeo money and attention. It's hard to have it all." Lucas stood up. "Thanks. I'll text you the time and restaurant. You're free tonight?"

"Sure, meet you there." Jack checked the time. "I have to update my files first."

On his way back to the break room, Ken caught Jack. "Time for a chat about that business?"

"What did you want to talk about?" Jack asked. He was already annoyed from going rounds with Lucas—that cowboy seemed to like a debate just to talk.

"An interview. I know you're not dressed for it," he said.

"Interview?" he asked.

Before, Ken had made it sound like it was Jack's to turn down.

"Yes, well, others might be interested. I have to be fair. You are the best, but I may not get the funding or investors. If I put you in charge of the staff while I run the business, that's not a real partnership but more of a promotion," he said.

"Right, a partnership would usually come with a buy-in of some amount. Credit or cash and then rights. We'd have to agree on things. Make decisions jointly. Doesn't seem like that's what you want anymore," Jack said.

He'd done his homework. The liability and so on weren't cheap. They got a deal being combined with a nursing home. Ken might be changing his mind.

Ken leaned back in his chair. "Don't put words in my mouth. I think Burrwood could use a standalone PT center, but then we're running our staff all over. Here, the home-bound visits, the other location and what if the hospital needs us to cover?"

"A lot of staff to manage, train and monitor. Do you have the patient load to cover it?" Jack asked.

"Projections indicate more PT will be needed with the aging population. But it might be best to promote someone to run the staff here, keep it centralized. Unless you've gathered enough funds," Ken said.

"I haven't explored my funds options yet. I'd need to see the terms, the offer and how much you're looking for from me. I know I could manage the staff, even though some are my friends, but if you want to keep control—then you need to figure out what changes will happen and how the business will look before you want any solutions from me."

"I did run a background check on you when I first hired you," Ken said.

"I'm sure," Jack replied.

"You have no student loan debt—your parents paid for your school?" he asked.

Jack sat up straighter. "No, I got a little help from scholarships and military options helped. I paid it all off. Why?"

"No, nothing. Just that your parents are known in Dallas to be business-minded. They might want to become investors," he said.

"No, you're not to contact my parents. I'm not interested in them putting up money to secure my position." Jack's parents had used money to manipulate things. They liked their status. Jack didn't want them using their money to somehow get a foothold in Burrwood and meddle.

Ken stood. "Now, that's not what I meant."

Jack stood as well. "I see. Well, when you have a better idea of what you mean and what you're offering, then we can do a more planned-out interview. If you don't know what job you're offering, I can't interview for it. But my parents won't be investing in your business attempts. I'll make sure of that."

Jack left, hoping he hadn't burned a bridge, but he wasn't going to do back flips and beg for a job when there was no information. One girl he'd worked with in Dallas had wanted a promotion so badly that her boss got her to do the job without it. He'd told her that if she took on the responsibilities, she might prove herself and then she could earn the title. What crap! Jack already went above and beyond to help his patients and co-workers but that was different. He'd mentor younger therapists, but when it came to his salary and benefits, Jack was a tough negotiator.

Jack had tried to warn his friend about being taken advantage of. That company had also played the *you know how little so and so makes* game to make others feel bad. Jack hadn't been able to believe it. His best advice was if a person doesn't value himself, the bosses certainly won't. People have to fight for themselves and what they deserve.

Getting into medicine to help people was nice, but it was still skilled work, not volunteering for a charity. He'd worked hard to pay off the student loans. Jack headed for the breakroom to get his things then head home.

"You okay?" Brenda asked.

"Fine. Just a long day. Night." Jack grabbed his bag, locked his locker and headed for the exit.

Was this what Lucas felt? Like people were looking past him to others, who might be easier to trick and use? Who might be younger? Who might be fools?

Jack didn't blame Lucas for wanting to hold on to his place. Jack wanted to keep his job too. Life dealt out changes and tests. Jack hoped that he hadn't stumbled onto one while helping Lucas through his.

The sudden urge to call him tingled through Jack's body. He got behind the wheel and started the engine. *No calling while driving.* It was a lame excuse, but it worked for now. He had to change for dinner anyway. He'd see Lucas soon enough.

* * * *

Lucas arrived early to settle in at the table. Jack showed up in a sport coat, like it was a date. Lucas' palms grew damp until he remembered his ex was coming too. He wanted a real date, but was it possible?

Suddenly he felt a bit underdressed. It was a nice restaurant but Lucas only wore jackets for very special occasions. Still, Lucas admired the effort. The feelings and conflicts in him were worse than any pain after his workout.

"Where's your ex?" Jack asked.

"Always fashionably late." Lucas reviewed the menu.

Jack glanced over his. "And this Al, you think he's innocent?"

"He's not the smartest guy. Good rider, good with the fans, and with the kids' group. He's been a bigger jerk than usual to me. I thought it might be competitive crap. Turns out, he's now dating Cathy. That's why he was squirrely. He thought I'd be pissed off," Lucas said.

"You seem relieved." Jack sipped his lemon water.

Lucas caught Jack's eye. "We dated for about six months. She's very nice," Lucas said.

He stood as he saw Cathy walking toward them. She was in a black dress chosen to make him regret letting her go and a silver necklace he'd bought her. Lucas didn't feel a twinge of loss or longing. His only regret was holding on to her when she could have been happier elsewhere.

*Even with Alvin.*

Jack stood as well.

"Cathy, hi. This is Jack, my PT expert. He's keeping me in line," Lucas introduced them.

"He's cute and a hunk! Shame I'm taken." Cathy air-kissed Lucas' cheek and shook Jack's hand before she sat down.

"Shame, but I'm gay," Jack said.

Lucas froze for a split second. Jack made it look so easy and casual.

"Then I'll just keep the man I'm with. He's definitely into women. You're in good shape, Jack, so you can get Lukey here back in tiptop form, I'm sure." Cathy grinned.

"Lukey?" Jack teased.

"That should stop since you're dating someone else, Cathy," Lucas said.

"Fine. I know Alvin has been weird but you and I were totally broken up before he made a move. Though I think he's been in love with me for like a year before that. I thought it was Pete at first, Al's weird friend—

he was always staring. Maybe he was a stalker or something. The rodeo brings all kinds, but no...Al is a good guy." Cathy opened her menu. "So Lucas will be fine?"

Jack nodded. "He'll recover from his injures. But it'll take a little time."

"Patient he is not," Cathy warned.

Jack smiled. "I figured that out. But the back can be tricky. Once injured, it can act up when strained."

"In rodeo terms, he should retire, but he's a stubborn bull who won't." Cathy smiled. "Why did you want to see me, Lucas? Alvin is good. He can't get enough of me and that includes my family dinners and taking me on the road with him. Stuff you never cared for."

"I'm happy for you. Truly, I'm not trying to interfere with you and Al. My fall, you didn't notice anything weird that night?" Lucas asked. Cathy had always wanted more time, more emotion, more sex and more of everything that Lucas just couldn't give her.

She frowned. Her blonde hair was twisted up off her neck so her long hoop earrings swayed when she shook her head. "No, nothing weird. But Al was occupying a lot of my time. I was trying to help fix up Pete. He had a few women he was interested in, but none worked out. One of my high school friends will be desperate enough when they show up for the reunion. I've got plans."

"Did you and Lucas have an amicable breakup?" Jack asked.

The waiter interrupted them and they ordered.

Cathy leaned in toward Jack after the waiter had left. "He was nice enough, if that's what amicable means. The chemistry had fizzled. Do you have a boyfriend? I have a cousin in Dallas. Hunky and a firefighter. I have his calendar at home—fundraiser to support their equipment needs. I can get you another one."

"Thanks, but I live here," Jack said.

"Why? You could have a better social life and job in the city. Small towns are awful on gays. As soon as my cousin turned eighteen, he bolted for the city. I'm going to get Al to move the minute he puts a ring on my finger," Cathy said.

"I grew up in Dallas. I liked it, but small towns have perks too. Do you know of anyone who might have wanted to sabotage Lucas' ride? Video shows the bull was acting a bit off," Jack said.

She turned her head and glared at Lucas, then tilted her head. "The mighty Lucas Burr couldn't have just fallen hard. *Noooo.* Someone must've tampered with the rig or the bull? Wow. You really think I did it?"

"No, I didn't say that. We were just going through a list of who might want to hurt me. I initiated the breakup. I wasn't a very good boyfriend," Lucas said.

"Both of those things are true. Still, I was ready to end that mess. He was all work and not a lot of time to be alone with me. Dinner with his mom or manager and friends. Tim needed a girlfriend, so tons of attempted double dates. With Pete, at least I can tell him to get lost and he does. Al wants me all to himself and alone as much as we can get," Cathy explained to Jack.

"No hard feelings. No harm wished on anyone. Great, one less suspect, but seriously, Cathy, if you know of anyone we should add to the list, please tell us. Getting Lucas healthy again only to have someone set him up again—it could end his life, not just his career," Jack said.

Cathy shrugged. "Plenty of people are competitive and jealous, but he owns part of the rodeo. If anyone was found out to be sabotaging the boss, they'd be blacklisted from every rodeo in Texas. Betray one rodeo owner, they'll *all* be worried about letting you ride. No one wants a crazy lawsuit or major tragedy in their ring."

"You really think no one in the rodeo wants him permanently out?" Jack asked.

"Maybe a few stupid ones, but they'd be too dumb to pull it off. Or they'd pay someone off to do it, like that hyper-religious right-wing investor y'all blocked out of buying into the rodeo. He'd pay someone, maybe. That someone would be smart enough to take the money and blow it off or do it and move to Arizona. Texas is big, but people run in small, tight circles. I'd look outside the rodeo circuit, but that's me," Cathy said.

Their food arrived and it occupied some of the silence for a bit. Lucas tried not to compare them in his mind. Cathy was nice, but Jack was attentive, smelled so good, looked like a dream in that jacket and was honest—no games, no tricks and no manipulation—not that any of it was Cathy's fault. Lucas wanted a man. Men were different—but Jack was better than any other guy he'd met yet.

"Jack, tell me who Lucas is dating now. No one seems to know," Cathy said as she finished her second glass of wine.

"I don't either. We mostly work out and discuss his medical recovery or the case. I've never seen him with a woman," Jack replied.

Lucas kicked Jack under the table.

"What a shame. But he's always micro-focused. This ride, this deal, the ranch this, this guy was a thief and so on. One day, he'll find someone he'll put everything else on the back burner for. She'll be a lucky girl." Cathy smiled and focused on her food.

"I'm sure you're right. I mostly see him in the office where it's not exactly social," Jack replied.

The tension was awkward. Lucas didn't see a future like Cathy had described. It wasn't just Cathy—no woman had ever felt like his future. He liked them but dating them always felt like a performance in the ring. He'd hang in there and it was a jolt of adrenaline but in the end, he knew he'd fall and run for the fence. No matter how many women, how hard he tried—Lucas felt like an idiot but he'd never wanted to give up on the hopes he'd be what his father wanted. It'd be easier. Why couldn't his life be easy?

Lucas tried not to stare at Jack, but he'd invited him because Jack made Lucas feel brave, calm and right. He felt right with Jack.

"Too bad Lucas isn't gay. You two are cute together. Good energy. Positive but calm. He was always so intense and antsy," Cathy said.

Lucas cleared his throat. "Don't start rumors."

"What? You're so paranoid. Maybe he has a sister or cousin like him at home with that same energy? You've always got to twist things and make a mountain out of an anthill." Cathy sighed. "Anyone else feel like dessert?"

Jack smiled and shot Lucas a look.

"The lady is always right," Jack said.

Lucas wanted to order five shots of whiskey, but he wouldn't. If he started drinking, he'd say the wrong thing or get too friendly with Jack. He had to be very careful. The attraction to Jack was ramping up and seeing him next to his last girlfriend only proved to Lucas what a fake he was.

# Chapter Ten

At the next PT session, Jack tried very hard to keep things professional with Lucas but being alone in the private room was too much temptation.

"Ready for another out-of-office adventure?" Jack asked.

Lucas brightened and looked him in the eye. "Hiking in the middle of nowhere again?"

"No, actually. Some walking will be involved, of course. It's good for you to be out not just hiding in here," he said.

He stood up on his own, straight without the slightest wince. "I'm good with it. Where?"

"It's a surprise. I'll drive." Jack put things in order then led Lucas out to his pickup.

Jack drove them to a mall one town over.

"A mall?" Lucas asked as they parked.

"Good for walking and I thought we could have lunch, talk about your suspects and that photo shoot," he said.

"Fine by me. There's a little Thai place in here I like but let's keep that between us," Lucas said.

They exited the car and headed for the entrance. "Why hide it?"

"I put it in an interview once and some guys questioned my native Texan status and other things. Like you can't try other foods but BBQ." He laughed.

"Good, I reserved a private booth in the back of that Thai place. But we have to walk all the way around the mall to get there." Jack went to the right.

The food place was just to the left, and the smell made him hungry, but Jack resisted.

"You are too smart. You read my mind or something? Jack, how do you know all my secrets?" he asked.

"I do my homework and it caught my eye. Sometimes I miss the diversity of Dallas. Small towns are safer and calmer but you have fewer choices. I'm sorry if I criticized your rodeo work. There aren't a ton of jobs in a small town and you're a big success." Jack picked up the pace a tad.

Lucas matched the stride. "I understand. It's not about the fame. My dad wanted to be known. I liked riding. I was good at breaking horses without getting hurt. There's an instinct for reading the animals and I had the gift. My uncle up in Nevada used to catch wild mustangs and tame them. Geld some of them and they were good horses for ranching and riding. Some he actually bred. One summer I went to stay with him and worked with horses. Best summer of my life."

"Is that why you rodeo with bulls? You want to tame the horses?" Jack asked.

His jaw tensed. "I like just ranching, but it's a rough way to make a living—so many ranches go under from one bad year. The rodeo makes people happy. It's a family night out. People need something to look forward to. Life is hard enough. This makes people happy."

"Family seems to make it worth it. You didn't want to settle down with Cathy?" Jack asked.

Lucas glared. "We didn't fit. Who knows why."

Jack grinned—he could tell Lucas was gay a mile away and that Lucas wanted Jack, not Cathy or any version of a woman under the sun. Lucas had to wrestle with his feelings until he could admit it and own it. "I could hazard a guess."

Lucas turned. "Don't. I'm not what you want me to be."

"I don't want you to be anything but who you are. Denying that sends a lot of people into therapy, pills for depression or worse. Like drinking to handle it."

"Everyone has problems. It's not all so cut and dried. We all have some wild oats to sow. Are you done with yours?" he teased.

"I had more than my share in the military and college. The freedom of being away from home and you can experiment. Isn't that what it's for?" Jack asked.

"Didn't go away for either. I'm definitely getting sick of bars and women only interested in the fame part of my life. The rest is as rough as everyone's," Lucas said.

"You never got away from the scrutiny of your parents. You always had their expectations in your face and pressing on you. And the rodeo life. Fame probably isn't all people imagine it to be. I've worked with athletes before. A few gymnasts dancers, football players. The pressure and attention make doing what they love and having a life hard." Jack led Lucas around a huge fountain.

Lucas paused and stretched his back a bit.

Jack noticed that they were alone and no one could see. That part of the mall was deserted—half the shops said closed, the others promised a new business coming soon. "Take your time. Is it hurting?"

"No, just a little tight. Stretching helps. You want to say you were right?" he asked.

"I'm always right about my business. I wouldn't tell you how to tame a horse," Jack teased.

Lucas smelled good and every time he leaned Jack's way, Jack stepped closer and tried to resist. Lucas had made it clear he was only interested in women but when they were alone and talking, it all felt different. Jack wanted to grab and kiss him. *Like teenagers making out at the mall.* He wanted to give Lucas what he'd never had, with guys anyway.

But he resisted, knowing Lucas would probably freak and it'd make lunch as awkward as hell. He stepped back and silently thanked his parents for living in Dallas. He'd grown up in a city where he could sneak into a gay bar and know he wasn't alone. His parents had never found out until he was ready to come out, and he'd had friends in the gay community so he'd known he wasn't alone.

"There is one really important fact that I need you understand before we get to the restaurant," Lucas said.

"What's that?" Jack locked eyes with Lucas.

"That I'm paying for lunch," he said joked.

The smile on Lucas' face told Jack few people ever said that to him. It was so easy to be with him. Jack couldn't keep to that 'friends' line. He grabbed and kissed Lucas before he could think or stop himself.

Lucas froze for a second, as if shocked, but he quickly pulled Jack in and deepened the kiss. Lucas felt as though they were melting into each other. Lucas took over and pressed Jack against the stone wall and Jack curled his arms around Lucas' neck. When Lucas slid his hands down and grabbed Jack's ass, Jack knew he hadn't been wrong about anything.

Lucas was in denial, but it wasn't his fault. Jack ran through what he knew about Lucas' story. Isolated in a small town, pressured into a masculine profession as a child in the rodeo and traveling around with his homophobic dad, the guy had never gotten a chance to explore. Even if he rodeo'd in a city, his dad had been right there, watching all the time. There had never been any running off to college or summer camp or anything—he'd been a rodeo cash cow and had to perform. If he'd sneaked off to a gay bar, someone would have seen. Hadn't Lucas said his dad had had pals all over the rodeo circuit and they'd have ratted Lucas out for the laugh…just to see his old man's face if he'd found out? He'd been conditioned to be what was safe—how did he break that without having a breakdown?

"We can't," Lucas said as he pulled away.

"Sorry, I didn't mean to." Jack followed him into the restaurant.

"It's not you. I did it too." Lucas took a deep breath.

Once at their table in the back, Jack waited for the lecture about how it'd never work.

"I can't seem to control myself. I don't want to give you mixed signals or the wrong idea," Lucas said.

"You never got to explore like a teen would. Your dad, the rodeo and the small town. Maybe that's what this is?" Jack suggested.

Lucas frowned and stared at the menu.

Jack wanted more, even if he got hurt. "Maybe you need to try it to see. You've spent so many years telling yourself that isn't you…the only way to know is to try."

"That's crazy," Lucas said.

"You don't have anything against other people being gay?" Jack asked.

"Of course not," Lucas insisted.

"Okay so why should you be so awful to yourself?" Jack asked.

"Don't do that," Lucas said.

"It was just a question. Maybe I'm not right about you. Then again, maybe I'm not Mr. Right. Maybe I'm the one you use to rule it out. A safe place to play." Jack had Lucas' attention now. He just left the topic.

"I don't want to use you or hurt you. I'm not going to screw up my career and get you fired for attraction and experimentation. My dad was so anti-gay and anti-everything that wasn't old-fashioned hardcore Texan that maybe it just appeals to me. I might just be a rebel," Lucas said.

Jack smiled. "I get it. I appreciate your concern for my job, but that's a temporary situation. You won't be my patient forever. I can wait to get you into bed. And if the pull is this intense for this long, it's not about your dead father. You're not fourteen, acting out with another rodeo kid under the stand."

"Thanks. I just need you to know I'm not trying to jerk you around. It's an active back and forth in my head. I'll land somewhere and figure out everything."

Lucas hoped he'd land before he ran out of air or lost his will to fight.

"Don't wait too long. Life is short." Jack sighed.

Lucas knew Jack was right. He just couldn't be like his dad and barrel through selfishly after what he wanted. His dad had never cared about other people, whether it was Mom wanting a dog or for her hubby to be home more—or Lucas wanting to be home more—what mattered was what Dad knew, thought and he was *always* right. Even if he wasn't.

But he was dead. Lucas had to find a way to silence that voice in his mind and decide what was right for himself.

* * * *

Full of Thai food and craving more of Jack, Lucas paced his home office. "Greg, I want to cancel the photo shoot. We can do an interview but I don't think the bull is a good idea."

Greg sat in the guest chair with his arms crossed. "It's a package promotional deal. They want your picture out there. It's good for the rodeo, good for business and good for you."

"How are they going to keep the bull still?" he asked.

"A vet gives them a little whatever. It chills them out. Doesn't hurt them. You'll be safe," Greg reassured him.

"Jack said I could sit as long as I took breaks to stretch out my back. Make sure I didn't put too much pressure for too long. But getting on and off a partially sedated wild animal…that's not smart," Lucas said.

Greg smiled. "Agreed. In that case, we do a quick shoot. One sitting."

"That won't look suspicious. They'll start asking more questions and pressing to see what I can do. It's too soon. I shouldn't have agreed to it. Let's say there's a conflict in scheduling and I'm going out of town. Kick it down the road a piece," he suggested.

"Then it does us no good. We need to keep you front and center. If we stall, they'll suspect things just like if you can't sit a bull for half an hour. You got pain pills you're not taking. Pop a couple for the shoot and then spend the rest of the day in bed with a heating pad. Tough it out—you're a pro," Greg said.

"I don't want to set myself back for the sake of promotion," he said.

"This is that PT guy. He said it was okay—you said so," Greg replied.

Lucas nodded. "But with breaks and I never said half an hour to him. I told you that but I got the sense you heard what you wanted to hear. That's how it usually works."

"I nudge you into what works. What is popular with fans and what you need to do. You love the animals and the rodeo part but the publicity and all that? You don't much care for that anymore," Greg replied.

They'd had this fight before but this was different. "Small doses of publicity are one thing but this is my health. My career depends on healing up right. Push it a bit if you can. Find a reason. I'm working as hard as I can but I'm not going to be trampled by or fall off a partially sedated bull during a photo shoot. That headline would really hurt business."

"Yeah, I suppose not." Greg shook his head.

"Or I could tell Mama and let her at you," Lucas warned.

Greg shifted in his seat. "I don't want to upset a lady. This is your career, not a time to run and hide behind your mama's skirts. Be a man."

Lucas had been hearing that since he was ten years old. *Don't cry. Be tough. Be a real cowboy.* Greg somehow brought up Lucas' father's ideals. The men had been friends and while Greg wasn't as aggressive, he was a constant reminder of the standard.

"Jack is a professional. He knows what he's doing better than we do," Lucas said.

"Well, the wheels are in motion. I'll do what I can, but figure it out," Greg said.

"I still feel like someone tampered with the bull or the ropes. It wasn't a normal fall," Lucas insisted.

Greg shook his head and sighed. "Don't be a crybaby. If someone was out for you, don't you think they'd do more than that?"

"I'm working through a list of suspects, no thanks to you. They might try again. Or maybe it was a spur-of-the-moment revenge impulse and they are over it? But what if it isn't about me? What if someone just wants to cause trouble, hurt animals or riders?" Lucas asked.

"We can up security around the riders and the animals, but you have to consider it was a fluke. The bull might've been fine then got worked up in the shoot. Maybe it kicked the gates and hurt itself on accident? Some are nastier kickers, some buck harder and that's the game of the rodeo." Greg leaned back.

"I know, I'm not trying to make it a big public thing. Oh, poor me… No, I'm not interested in sympathy. I just want to know the people and animals are safe at our ring," Lucas explained. He couldn't open a proper investigation because of the attitudes just like that.

"Fair enough. I'll have security and handlers keep an eye out for meddling. If you want to hunt down your old grudges, fine. But get your head back in the game. Publicity, interviews and so on until we can get you back in the rodeo," Greg said.

"And finish PT," Lucas said.

"Sure. It looks good for the kids and so on," Greg replied.

"Great." Lucas was pulled in so many directions that he felt lost in his own life. Before Jack, Lucas had known something was missing—now he had the pieces but wasn't sure any of them would fit right. Before Greg had seemed in favor of PT, but it was a dog and pony show that fit into the comeback story he wanted to sell.

Lucas felt like he'd let Jack down. The kiss had been great and he wanted more. The lunch had only been tense for a short while and then they'd fallen into childhood stories of Texas. He had plans for them—he wanted to see Jack on a horse.

He wanted to be invited to one of Jack's family Sunday dinners.

He wanted a lot of new things now that Jack had come into his life. But as friends. Experimenting and fooling around? Lucas wanted that too but maybe it was just wild oats? He didn't want to hurt Jack in the process.

Something deep down told Lucas that was a crock.

Jack was no oat.

# Chapter Eleven

Lucas wasn't afraid to fall. He made a living from it. Falling off the bull, getting back on another night—surviving was winning. Whatever Jack wanted to throw at him, he'd survive this fight.

He made it up the stairs to Jack's apartment without pain. Things were improving. He knocked on the door and waited. He knocked again, ready to call Jack's phone to see if he was at home.

The door opened and Jack's face was so serious that Lucas forgot what he was going to say.

"Hi," he said.

"Hi. What are you doing here?" Jack asked.

"Can I come in?" he asked.

"How did you find my address?" Jack countered.

"Small towns, no secrets." He smiled. "We need to talk."

"Oh, I thought you got drunk again and wanted someone to make you feel better." Jack folded his arms.

Lucas shook his head. "No, we need to talk about the mall."

"I'm sorry about that," Jack said softly. "I'm not used to hiding or being with guys who are in the closet. Get in here before the neighbors get too nosy."

Lucas walked in and Jack closed the door. Looking around the apartment, Lucas had expected nothing less. *Neat and tidy.* He had a dark green couch and beige side chairs, and the windows were all open letting in sun and fresh air.

A little dog ran up and yapped.

"That's Roscoe. He's all bark." Jack headed for the kitchen. "Coffee? Water?" he offered.

"Either is fine. I tried to cancel the promotional photo shoot. Hopefully I managed at least to push it off a bit," he said. "Hi, Roscoe."

"Good. It won't set you back too much, but you'll feel it. I just don't trust a bull, sedated or not. I'm not trying to hurt your career," Jack said.

"I never thought you were. Why the sudden chill?" he asked.

Jack handed him a cup of coffee. "You're my patient. I can't… That kiss was wrong. You made the other moves but it never went far. I can't screw up my career like that. I promise it won't happen again and we won't do any more sessions outside of the PT office."

That was the wrong direction. "I don't want that."

"You don't get a choice. I was weak. If you want to fire me, go to someone else, or sue the office—it's up to you." Jack leaned back on the counter.

"I'm not suing anyone. I'm not upset that you did it—just where. I don't want anyone else." How could he explain this? With Jack around, Lucas didn't want to go to the bars and find random women to admire him. He didn't need to show off on the mechanical bull or with a photo shoot.

"We need to keep our relationship strictly professional," Jack said.

"No one ever said I was a bad kisser, but you did catch me off guard." Lucas hadn't dealt with much rejection in his life, but his ego could take a 'no thanks, I'm married, I've got a boyfriend or I'm not interested'. He respected women.

Jack laughed. "It wasn't bad. But I'm not risking my career. Men get fixated on caretakers. It happens. Nightingale syndrome. I've never given into it because I know it's temporary. It's not real. It rarely happens with a male caretaker though. Well, mostly it's doctors. Maybe becoming too friendly but not the romantic attachment. You're a tough case and I projected weird feelings onto you. I'm thrilled you're cooperating and seeing progress with the therapy but as you recover, you won't need me. The attachment goes away and you go back to your life. Your female entourage. I shouldn't have crossed the line."

"You'll move on to other patients and care for them. I'll be forgotten," Lucas said.

He'd been kicked a couple of times by a pissed-off horse. Jack dismissing Lucas felt worse than a kick. Like anytime he was thrown, he tried to find his footing, but it wasn't his back or legs giving him trouble—it was his insides. Before he'd always managed to take rejection with his head held high, but this gutted him.

"You look like you're in pain. You can sit, if it'll help," Jack offered.

"It's not my back. This isn't Nightingale whatever. I'm not a kid or clueless. This isn't the first time I've been hurt. I was in the hospital for a week. I had plenty of pretty nurses and some were fans," he said.

"Maybe you should call them up then?" Jack suggested.

"What?" He shook his head. "Why?"

"You're not their patient anymore so they can date you now. I get it—the photo shoot and going out to bars. You want to look like you're back in the saddle with women and your career." He grabbed his own mug of coffee and sipped.

Lucas moved into the kitchen but kept a safe distance. He'd never seen Jack this wound up. He looked ready to throw a punch. "Don't you think you've had enough coffee?"

Setting the mug down sharply, Jack glared at him. "It's not the caffeine. I've worked very hard to get to where I am in my career. It might not be much in a small town but it's important to me. I did it on my own and I'm not going to screw it up by crossing lines with patients. I can't. I never have until you. It's not your fault. It's mine," he said.

"No, it's mine. I made the first moves. I wanted to kiss you from the first time I saw you. That's why I wanted someone else, but I really didn't because PT was an excuse to be around you without dealing with my crap. I'm not attracted to every guy on the planet. Some, yeah, but you're different. I can't resist. You're smart, confident and wouldn't fall for the charming cowboy crap. I'm sorry I hurt you and I'd never say anything happened while I was your patient. I don't want to hurt your career," he said with a smile. The emotions swirled internally—hope and hurt mixed with the ever-present fear.

"Right, you knew all of that the first time you met me?" Jack scoffed.

"I did. You were out so there was no chance of anything more because that's not my life. But I'd be an idiot and cross the lines. I knew that much," he said.

"Oh please, you didn't want people judging you because I was gay," Jack argued.

Smiling, Lucas moved closer. "All right, you win. I felt like everyone was watching me looking at you. I've fallen off in the rodeo plenty of times but never landed that long in the hospital. I never had that fear that I would never walk. I never limped so much in my life. I hated my mother and the other rodeo ladies seeing me like that. I hated anyone seeing me like that. And just when I start recovering, I meet this hot guy who is down to earth and doesn't really know or care about the rodeo world."

"I can move you to another physical therapist," Jack offered.

Lucas shrugged. If that was the only solution that Jack was comfortable with, he'd take it. He wanted the best and that was still Jack...other perks aside.

"Then we don't have to see each other anymore and it'll all just go away." Jack picked up his phone like he was going to text the request right now.

"What? No." Lucas grabbed Jack's phone and chucked it onto the sofa to buy himself a little time. Roscoe barked and ran after the phone "I don't want that. I want more time with you, not less. PT or personal, I'll work with whatever you give me but I want more of what we did at the mall by that fountain. Not less. You're the best physical therapist in the state, Everyone says so. I want the best. We can handle this for the short term. Professional in the office and careful outside so no one knows until I'm not your patient. I swear."

"You're not going to freak out and push me away again?" Jack asked.

"All yours." Lucas worked Jack's fly without an ounce of shame.

Jack pulled Lucas into the bedroom and closed the door before Roscoe followed.

Lucas smiled. He didn't need a little dog for an audience.

Their shirts were tossed to the floor as Jack opened Lucas' jeans and pushed his pants down then eased him to sit on the bed.

"I'm fine." Lucas stroked Jack's cock and kissed his neck.

"I know, but I want you good to go all night." Jack tugged Lucas's jeans and boxers all the way off.

The men locked eyes and Lucas should've felt vulnerable. Instead he felt free and safe. This was how it was supposed to feel. He pulled Jack to him and kissed the man who'd found a way to break through all the fear and defenses Lucas had piled up.

Jack kissed him back then worked his hot mouth and tongue down Lucas' chest. When Jack started sucking Lucas's cock, he grabbed Jack's hair. "No, I want all of it. Not just messing around."

"I promise, you'll get it. Which way?" Jack teased Lucas' balls then went behind.

Lucas tensed for a second but those skilled fingers playing with his asshole made him surrender. "That, you inside of me."

"You are full of surprises today." Jack eased Lucas all the way on the bed and went right back to work blowing Lucas' brains out.

"Stop, what, what are you doing? I want…" Lucas wanted both but he wanted to get Jack off too.

"I know. Relax." Jack sucked the tip of Lucas' cock and fingered his ass until Lucas tensed in orgasm.

"Jack!" Lucas was shaking as Jack swallowed the load, not missing a drop.

"That's insane," Lucas muttered.

"That's just the beginning." Jack opened the drawer on the nightstand and produced a condom and a lube packet.

Guiding Lucas until he was flat on his back, Jack kissed him slowly.

"Missionary with a guy," Lucas mumbled against Jack's mouth.

Jack grinned and tore open the lube. "It's good. When your back is fully healed, you can get as creative as you want."

Lucas exhaled slowly as Jack lubed him. He'd dreamed of it but—"I've never..."

"I know. I'll be gentle." Jack teased a finger inside his hot cowboy.

"At first maybe but fuck no—I just want to be with you." Lucas grabbed the condom and opened it.

Nodding, Jack helped Lucas get that in place. "Relax."

Lucas wrapped his legs around Jack's waist and pulled close. His erection was bigger than a finger but the lube and arousal made Lucas crave more. When Jack pulled back, Lucas groaned.

"I need you," Lucas said.

Jack kissed him and filled him deeper this time. "I need you too, but I won't hurt you. Soon you'll be able to ride me like a horse and take it however hard and fast you want."

Moaning, Lucas lifted his hips.

Jack groaned. "First time, really." Jack thrust in fully.

"Mine, you're mine." Lucas arched his back. His hips worked and his muscles tightened on Jack's cock.

"Mine," Jack whispered back as his thrusts founds a pattern. Lucas surrendered to their connection and the pressure built.

"Jack," Lucas groaned.

"It's okay," Jack reassured him.

"I'm right there. A little faster, please," he said.

Jack shifted his weight just a bit and the pace ramped up. Lucas rocked to meet him but they only stayed on that edge for a few moments before the orgasm hit him like a stampede. He screamed Jack's name and held on to him. Jack lasted a few more thrusts before he ground and pressed.

"You okay?" Lucas asked Jack.

Jack laughed and looked up. "That's my line." They kissed and feel into a sleepy haze.

Jack nuzzled Lucas' shoulder after they'd both had some time to recharge. It almost didn't feel real, but it was. Jack disposed of the used condoms and cleaned up a bit but Lucas hadn't dozed well without Jack there.

"I've never done that before," Lucas admitted.

Jack smiled. "Being on the receiving end?"

"Either. I always limited it to hand or blow jobs. But it was random hookups and they were rare." Lucas traced over Jack's tattoo.

"Regrets?" Jack asked.

Lucas shook his head. "No. Well, maybe that I waited. I just don't… It makes no sense. I didn't hate it with women."

Jack grinned and shifted. When Lucas tried to shift, Jack pushed him to stay flat on his back. Jack half pinned Lucas with his body and snuggled chest-to-chest. "I'm not bothered if you're bi. But you can't have one of each at the same time."

Lucas laughed. "No, I couldn't handle that. Rodeo is half sport and half a show. You're putting on a performance to a point—at least the good ones are."

"Looking all tough and fearless while making it look rough," Jack teased.

Lucas nodded. "Exactly."

"If you say this was acting, I'll tie you to the bed and prove it wasn't until you admit it." Jack slid his hand down Lucas' hairy chest and the naturally developed abs to torment his cock to attention.

"Stop, this was not an act. The women feel like they were, now." Lucas shook his head.

Jack kissed Lucas' neck. "It doesn't all come clear at once. But you seem clearer."

They kissed slowly. Jack wanted to dive in and let all his feelings loose but it'd scare Lucas and he'd run.

"This would change everything." Lucas closed his eyes.

"This?" Jack prompted.

"Us. I don't know how. I'm not sure I can," he said.

Jack's chest hurt. "You're brave enough to ride a wild bull that could kill you but afraid of what people think if you're dating me?"

"Jack, don't," Lucas said.

"I'm serious. Think about that. You're not scared of anything. Not really. You do this crazy crap and that's socially acceptable because it's manly and dangerous. You're brave enough to do that, so what can't you do?" Jack asked.

"It'd damage my career." Lucas sighed. "That's not up for debate."

"No such thing as bad press. I look good in pictures." Jack dropped kisses over Lucas' neck and chest.

"Stop. I can't move as fast as you." Lucas started to sit up.

Jack rubbed Lucas' neck. "It's okay. I'm not asking you to do anything. I'm teasing."

Lucas looked him in the eye. "You know who you are and what you want. I envy that but I'm not there yet."

"Okay, I can respect that. But I think you know yourself more than you think. It's about you. You just have to trust yourself. Don't do anything for me," Jack said.

Lucas frowned. "I'm not sure I know how to do that."

"Mom, Dad, Greg and your brothers? Fans? Business partners? Rabid female admirers? Who else are you living your life for?" Jack asked.

"It's not that bad." Lucas sighed.

"Whatever you say." Jack kissed him and reached for another condom and lube packet. "Now we could keep debating things or put your erection to good use. Or if you want to take it again, I'm ready when you are."

Lucas grinned. "I want to watch you ride my cock."

"Sounds good to me. You do the honors." He tossed Lucas a lube packet.

Adjusting his pillows so he could see and wasn't lying totally flat, Lucas tore open the packet. Jack turned his back on Lucas to slide the condom on his dick.

Lucas played with the lube a bit and worked some into Jack's ass. "You look amazing naked."

"So do you." Jack stroked Lucas' balls.

Lucas lifted his hips but smacked Jack on the ass. "I want this all the time."

"Me too." Jack kissed Lucas' upper inner thighs. "Slap my ass again."

Lucas did it without question and Jack groaned. "You like it rough in the ring? Maybe I like it a little rough in bed."

"I'm not paying you to ride my dick," Lucas teased.

Jack turned around and braced his hands on Lucas' chest. "Don't make fun."

"I'm not. I don't know how to do that." Lucas gasped as Jack eased down on his erection and took it all on the first stroke.

"Shit," Lucas said.

"Want me to slow down?" Jack leaned in and kissed him.

Lucas reached a hand around and slapped that butt like it was a bull's rump in a rodeo. "No, ride me however you want. Use me." He gripped Jack's cock with his other hand and stroked.

"Lucas, you're going make me lose it too fast." Jack tried to push his hand away.

Decreasing the pressure on his cock, Lucas gave Jack another hard slap on the rear. The groaning and how Jack tightened on Lucas' dick told him he was doing it right.

"More of that?" Lucas teased.

Jack nodded as his hips snapped down faster. Lucas grabbed Jack's ass with both hands and squeezed those firm cheeks before slapping them both at the same time.

Jack ground down and pressed.

"Are you coming on my dick?" Lucas asked.

"A little. I'm far from done with you." Jack kissed Lucas' grinning mouth.

Jack licked his way down and bit Lucas' nipple until he groaned. That got him another slap on the rump. The tingling and the sting of pain made him harder. It'd never worked out before where a guy he liked—hell, that he loved—always wanted to play rough.

"Bad boy," Lucas said in Jack's ear.

"I'm not into like hardcore BDSM. I'm not that kinked out, I swear," Jack confessed.

Lucas smiled. "It's okay. I had a few girlfriends who were. It was easier to play along when I knew what she wanted and had control. It was hot but not like this. Ropes, leather, spanking—whatever you want."

Jack gave Lucas' other nipple a teasing nibble. "What do you want?"

"This, but more. All of it. I want to fuck you, ride you, spank you and suck your dick." Lucas thrust up.

"Jerk me off," Jack said.

"Nah, I want to see you blow on your own. Ride me." Lucas smiled.

Jack leaned back and found the perfect angle, riding that long cock, his own erection bobbing.

"Please, Lucas," Jack groaned.

"So close, I can feel it." Lucas rubbed his fingers over Jack's cock and teased the tip.

"I want you to come first," Jack said.

Lucas laughed. "Nope, you." He gently smacked Jack's cock.

"Fuck, Lucas!" Jack trembled and sank back down on his dick.

"You like more than your ass spanked." Lucas slapped Jack's cock gently in time with the riding and it only took two times before Jack screamed and ground down. The cum shot from his cock all over Lucas and only then did he stroke Jack properly—if a bit roughly.

Lucas lifted his hips, fucking Jack as he shuddered in orgasm. "Mine," Jack whispered.

"All yours, but you're due a proper spanking for keeping this slightly kinky side from me. Nothing a cowboy loves more than roping and riding bareback." Lucas kissed him.

Jack floated in the sweet space of orgasm and safety. It couldn't be real…but it was.

# Chapter Twelve

Stretching out in Jack's bed, Lucas hadn't felt this good—ever. He couldn't remember a moment where he'd been this content and happy. When he reached over and found the bed empty, he realized the shower was on. He did tend to sleep like the dead.

Grabbing his phone, he checked the time. It was late and a workday. Jack had a job to go to. Lucas didn't want to screw that up for him any more than their public kiss might. That part of the mall was abandoned so Lucas convinced himself no one could've seen it.

He'd always imagined panicking and shame after he actually crossed the line with a guy. It was completely different. He didn't feel urge to be alone and hop in the shower. Well, right now the shower would be fun because Jack was in there.

He rolled over to Jack's pillow and inhaled. They had more things to talk about but their hormones had gotten in the way. His phone binged and Lucas wanted to throw it out of the window. The whole world could go away for a few days and let them be happy—and sort things out before anyone else knew.

It was probably his mom or Greg.

He grabbed the phone and looked at it.

A text in all caps from Greg telling him the photo shoot had been moved up to today, like it or not. Take it or leave it.

Lucas wanted so badly to leave it but he knew how that would look. If they canceled promotional stuff, it'd look like they were hiding something…and not just him sleeping with his physical therapist. The speculation about his condition and the future of his career would hurt far worse than sitting on a bull for a bit could. He'd power through and if the pain was bad, take one of the prescription pain killers after. He texted Greg.

*Slept late, OMW. Be there in 20*

He had to text Jack too.

*Photo shoot moved to this morning. I'll be careful. Talk soon…*

Anything more felt like he was moving too fast and would promise too much. Or it might come off as overexplaining himself. He wasn't the savviest texter in the world. He wanted to say a lot more but even thinking it scared him.

Hopping out of bed, he threw on his clothes then shoved his feet into the boots. The afterglow had him pain-free at a new level. He waited a moment but the shower was still going. Finally, he had to go. Lucas exited out of the front door and made it sure it locked behind him and Roscoe didn't sneak out.

An hour later he was watching a vet try to stick a needle in a bull's tail. He'd put his foot down about mild sedation. Especially since the promo people wanted a long-horned bull for the shoot.

The photographer came over. "You know, we don't mind an action shot. If you want to ride."

Lucas shot Greg a look.

"That's not possible," Greg said.

"So, Mr. Burr won't ride again or can't?"

"No, he's not cleared medically to ride rodeo yet," Greg corrected.

Lucas sighed. "This is my ranch, gentlemen. My personal home. It's not set up for rodeoing. We don't have safety guys or that level of liability insurance to rodeo. I'm especially not going against doctor's orders. There's no such thing as a tame bull, especially with a set of horns like that. You can't expect them to stand still while someone sits on them and a bunch of others watch, talk and photograph things."

"The sedative will do the trick," Greg said.

"Or we could use a horse that is actually tame and I could ride that if you want more action," Lucas suggested.

"That visual would lack impact. A cowboy on a horse isn't dangerous. Besides, he's known to ride bulls in the rodeo. We need him in a blue flannel shirt, open at the neck and a cowboy hat." The photographer patted Lucas' shoulder.

Lucas glared at Greg. "Fine, I'll change."

"Be positive. Act like a success and not like a defeated loser," Greg scolded.

"I'm recovering. In the middle of it isn't the best time to take a victory lap," Lucas shot back.

He changed and climbed on the bull using a step ladder. The bull moved and snorted, but was too slow to escape. Settling in, Lucas wanted this over ASAP.

"Are you excited about getting back in the rodeo?" the interviewer asked.

"Can't wait. Working hard every day for a complete recovery. If only I could get myself better than I was before," Lucas teased.

"Any special events planned for your return?" The interviewer tossed a softball question at them.

"I'm planning on my home turf unless I get a better offer," Lucas replied.

Greg cleared his throat. "We are taking offers, of course."

Lucas' back ached as the photographer and interviewer packed up. The ranch hands brought the step ladder over and helped Lucas off the bull, who was now fighting to recover from the sedative.

Lucas slipped as he hit the ground, but his hands steadied him. His back and legs weren't totally numb despite being stiff from that position. That was definitely progress. There was no chance to celebrate, though—the bull stomped the dirt with his front right hoof.

"Out of the pen," Greg advised.

Lucas rushed, feeling the strain in his lower back. The bull was kicking out his back hooves and running off to charge anything in sight within a minute of the men clearing the fence.

Mama walked out on the porch. "Lunch is ready if you want to stay, Greg."

"No, I think I stirred up enough trouble today. Thanks." Greg headed for his pickup.

"Boys, wash up, now," Mama said.

"Not me, I'm heading to bed to rest my back. I'll eat later, thanks." Lucas tried to walk normal and steady.

"I can get your cane," she offered.

"No, thanks." He headed straight to his room and flopped face down.

What he would've given right then to have Jack appear and put some of that cream with pain reliever on his lower back. Then they could have fun. Not that he'd be able to move much but he could certainly entertain him even if this position.

He fished his phone from his pocket, tossing the cowboy hat in the corner. Before calling Jack, he checked for texts or voicemails. Nothing. Dashing out and leaving a text was not a great start but they both had to work. Schedules changed. He'd understand.

Wouldn't he?

Lucas got through to Jack's voicemail.

"Hey, Jack, I'm sorry about this morning. Believe me, I didn't want to leave at all. I made it through the photo shoot and my back is stiff and sore as expected. I'm going to cave and take one of those pain pills but that's it. Tomorrow I'll be at physical therapy but I might be a lot stiffer than normal. Don't worry, okay—all professional at work. But I will ask you out on a date in private if you don't call or text me back with an answer to this invitation. A real date, Jack. We're grown-ups, I'm sure you're not supposed to date your patients, but I'm not terminal. I've only got a few more weeks of it. If I have to wait that long for the date, fine. I will…but I want a chance to take you out. And it's not a thank you for helping me or anything. That's just your job, right? I'm rambling, sorry. The pain. I should probably eat something before I take the pill. I'm not drunk but I feel tired. I didn't drink any water while I was on the bull sitting in the sun and out there. I need water, that's it. Sorry, just call me back, okay?" he asked than added hastily, "It's Lucas."

He ended the call. "I'm an idiot."

There was a tap on his door. "Food coming to you."

"Mama, you don't have to." His stomach disagreed.

"Baked potato, spare ribs with your favorite sauce, and corn on the cob. Biscuits and butter. I brought a beer but I think you need water."

"Yeah, thanks. I need two big glasses of water, if you don't mind. I'm going to take one of those pills so the pain goes away, eat and rest so that I can work out tomorrow," he said.

"Sounds sensible." She set the tray down.

"Thanks, take the beer away. I'm not mixing that with the pill." He smiled.

"Good. Got the pills?" she asked.

"I think put them in the bathroom cabinet. Do you mind?" he asked.

"Don't stay in one position again. You'll just freeze up your back all over." She handed him one pill. "I'll get the water but if you want dessert, you can venture out to us."

"Thanks, I will. I'm due for an anti-inflammatory too." He reached for his bottle on the nightstand. "Got it."

"Good, eat before it gets cold. I'll get you lots of water." Mama headed out.

He knew he'd need help. Everyone did from time to time. His ego was a bit bruised having to rely on his mother but if he'd ended up in a wheelchair or with any level of paralysis, he'd only be more dependent on others.

He got another chance at life and he wasn't going to be all work and no play—even if he enjoyed his work, there was more to life than horses and rodeo.

* * * *

On his lunch break, Jack listened to the message from Lucas. Part of him wanted to grin like a teenager. Another part of him wanted to leave early and go to Lucas' house. The reality was that that was a bad idea. None of Jack's neighbors had mentioned anything or texted so far. They weren't prudes or overly nosy but small towns only had so many apartment buildings and the people looked out for one another.

"What's wrong, Jack?" Teddy asked as Jack put his phone down.

"Nothing. I was just thinking of old Mr. Gruber," she said.

"He's doing fine. You can take the nursing home rounds any day," Brenda offered.

"Thanks, when Lucas is off my plate, I absolutely will. He's doing better now that he's cooperating," he said.

"Well, Mr. Gruber has made friends. The old ladies love him. He's strong but those stairs at his old apartment building were hard for him to manage. Maybe if a first-floor unit had opened up he could've managed to stay on his own longer. But he's probably better off where he is. Mid-seventies, having the help on hand if he needs it is good," Brenda said.

"I'm glad. I miss him around the apartments but it's safer for him." Jack focused on his lunch, but the truth was he'd only thought of Mr. Gruber because he didn't want to end up like him. Alone, never married, working and doing all the routine stuff of life alone. One day, he'd fallen on the stairs and there'd been no one to call.

Not wanting to be alone was not a reason to go after Lucas. But Jack hadn't worried about things like that before. He could grow old with his cousins and be the fun uncle to their kids. Or find a nice guy like Mark and it might be enough. He'd always have family around. A man was only great if he was the right one.

"He's lost again," Teddy said.

"I'm here. Just thinking," Jack replied.

"You feel okay?" Teddy asked.

His phone rang. "Yeah, I'm just not hungry." Jack answered her phone to avoid more chitchat.

Teddy tossed his trash and left the break room.

"Is this Jack Gable?" someone asked.

"Speaking." It was probably a sales call. He should've looked at the ID but he wanted to stop the random work conversations before he said too much about Lucas.

"My name is Heather from a local newspaper here in Texas. We'd love to get an exclusive interview with you," she said.

"What newspaper? Why?" Jack asked.

"Well, it's more of an online presence now but we still are in some big cities for delivery. We'd love to talk about your relationship with Lucas Burr," Heather dodged the question.

"You want to talk about physical therapy? What's the name of your paper and your full name?" Jack pressed.

"I'm Heather Anderson with the *Texas Tattler*. People just love rodeo and Lucas is a small-town hero turned big celebrity. You're the man bringing him back to life in more ways than one. We'd really make it worth your time for an exclusive with pictures," she said.

"Worth my time?" he repeated.

"We pay for exclusivity and details. We know you two are more than friends," she said.

"You've got the wrong person. Don't call this number again," Jack said.

Ending the call, he stared at his phone in disbelief. Who would know? How would they know?

He shook his head. "They were just fishing for a story."

His phone rang again from the same number.

He answered. "I said don't call me again."

"I understand but you need to know. We have pics of you two kissing at a mall and of him coming out of your apartment building very early in the morning. It won't help your career. Give us a good story where he crossed the line and seduced you and we'll make sure you look like the victim to his charming cowboy ways. The money will help you if you get let go. If you don't cooperate, you're the one who seduced his patient while he's weak and in pain." Heather's cold tone sent a chill through Jack.

"Why are you after him?" Jack asked.

"We're after a good story. No one cares if a guy is sleeping around with women. We have plenty of pics of him in bars kissing random women and dancing. But a secretly gay rodeo star? You're a good guy with a good job and he's using you for his dirty little secret."

"Being gay isn't dirty," Jack shot back.

"I know. You're out and respected. No reputation or any exes out to talk about you. We'll show Lucas for the user and heartbreaker he is. He's ashamed of what you have. Is he promising you something real? Because he's not the type who'll ever come out. It'd ruin his life and career. We can tell this right and make you the favorite physical therapist in all of Texas. Dirty rodeo cowboy on the downlow breaks the heart of the angel who healed him. This could get us record downloads."

"I'm not interested," Jack said.

"We haven't talked numbers yet. If you have pics of Lucas naked, I could get you a tiny cut of the profits per download," she offered.

"No means no. Don't call again." Jack pinched the bridge of his nose and whispered, "Oh my God."

# Chapter Thirteen

After two more PT appointments, Jack was still staying strictly professional and Lucas appreciated it. As much as he wanted more, he knew they were rarely alone and the wrong impression getting out would hurt both of their careers. PT just had to end and then it could change.

But the fact that Jack wasn't making an effort to be alone with Lucas and wasn't even really talking to him made Lucas miserable.

Lucas returned to an old habit of helping muck the stalls and feed the horses for some useful exercise first thing in the morning. It helped him think. Then he headed in for breakfast.

Today he found Greg at the table enjoying his mom's French toast.

"Morning," Greg said.

"Morning. What brings you here so early?" Lucas asked.

"The story about you hit last night online and it got picked up by all the local papers this morning. I was already getting texts last night and a few calls this morning. People want you back on the rodeo circuit. Even if you're not riding competitively, you can be part of the grand parade in," Greg suggested.

"Please, they want to see him ride," Mama replied.

"Ideally, when he's ready. But he can award prizes, show people he can still sit a horse and set an example," Greg countered.

Lucas ate and considered the options. "I haven't been cleared to ride horses yet."

"This PT dude is slowing things down. When do you see your doc again?" Greg asked.

Mama poured more coffee. "Don't rush him."

"It can't hurt to ask the doctor. Don't they re-scan you every so often?" Greg asked.

"I'll call and see the doc." Lucas didn't want a fight.

"What's got you tense?" Mama asked.

"Nothing new. I want to get back to normal but rushing it could ruin my future and everyone thinks they know the proper timetable," Lucas replied.

"Call the doc and get the proper timetable. The PT guy is good, smart, but he's not a doctor. We got you one of the best ortho guys in the state. You'll have to go to him in Houston but that's okay. Make the appointment. I'll arrange for us to meet with the rodeo guys after you've seen the doc." Greg put his phone down.

Mama sat down. "Isn't this nice? A family breakfast."

* * * *

After the doctor, Lucas impulsively swung by the ranch where the bull was kept. The hands acted oddly, but the owner didn't seem to be bothered.

"See, he's fine." The owner shook Lucas' hand.

"I do. Glad to know it. It was a weird ride and a bad fall. It happens to all of us but it felt like more." Lucas adjusted his hat.

The owner chuckled. "You don't get to be rich and famous without being a target. Owning a ranch and a piece of a rodeo is enough. I don't blame you. Greg said he's upping security around the animals. Sounds good to me. We've all got enemies out there."

"Good to know you don't think I'm totally paranoid," Lucas said.

"Nah. But you have to learn to ignore it. You have to be above it, unless you can prove it. If you can prove it, put 'em in jail but if you can't, don't whine. People hate whiney rich guys." The owner chuckled.

"I'm not whining. We run a sloppy rodeo where people get hurt and we're out of business. Nothing is perfect but I want high standards," Lucas replied.

"You got 'em. Most people respect and appreciate it. Some will always scoff and critique." The owner checked his phone. "I've got a conference call I need to hop on. You good?"

"Fine, thanks. I'm leaving." Lucas shook his hand.

"You can hang around if you want. But rumor is it you'll be back in the saddle soon. I'm sure you've got practice and work to do." The owner nodded and headed away.

* * * *

That evening, Lucas felt better having gotten away. The doctor had fitted him in at the drop of a hat. That had surprised Lucas, but his minor celebrity seemed to work in his favor. Greg had appointments lined up for tomorrow but tonight Lucas kept for himself.

Jack still wasn't taking his phone calls. But he had his own job to do with PT appointments. Still, Lucas had never been the one left out there hanging, wondering.

*It sucks.*

Parking his truck outside a steakhouse, he sat there for a minute. Tim's truck was already there. He needed a real friend, not drinking buddies, tonight.

As he walked through the packed main room, he spotted Al and Cathy. He detoured and tipped his hat.

"What a coincidence. Gotta a secret girl?" Al asked.

"Not unless you count Tim, but I'd never sleep with him," Lucas joked.

Cathy smiled. "That'd be something to see."

"Hey, Al, quick question. Do you know where that ranch hand I had to fire last year for stealing ended up working?" Lucas asked.

"Mexican or the one white?" Al asked.

"White guy, Donnie Smith—poor Paco ended up caught by ICE," Lucas replied.

"Damn. No, I don't think I've heard about Donnie but he wasn't much in the rodeo. He liked keeping to himself with the ranch work. If I hear anything, I'll let you know," Al said.

"Thanks. I'll let you get back to it. But I wanted to say I'm glad you two are still together. And to reiterate my warning, Al, If you don't treat her right, you'll answer to me," Lucas said.

"Such a true-blue cowboy. I wouldn't dream of it." Al reached out and took Cathy's hand. There was a diamond ring on it.

"Congrats! Wow." Lucas shook Al's hand.

"When you know you know." Cathy beamed.

Lucas gave her a peck on the cheek. "Keep him in line."

"Will do. You'll be invited. Can't wait to see who is your plus one," Cathy said.

"Thanks, I can't wait. Tim's waiting somewhere. I'll leave you two to celebrate." Lucas headed for the back room. He found Tim in a back booth.

"Hey." Lucas sat down.

"Hey. You okay?" Tim asked.

"Sure, Cathy and Al are sitting out there and engaged. So that was a surprise. Why?" Lucas asked.

Tim sat back. "I haven't heard from you in a while. Word is you were hanging with Al, Pete and mostly Jack. You look a little off."

"Are you jealous?" Lucas teased.

"Please. You want to play with those two goofs, fine. Jack, I don't know the guy but you know what people will say. I knew you'd come back to your real friends but it took you long enough," Tim said.

"I'm sorry. Seriously, I need a real friend now. There's another reason I didn't want to bug you," Lucas said.

"You and a new girl?" Tim guessed.

"No. Not a girl. Jack. I couldn't... He's not responding to my texts or anything. I think I blew up my life," Lucas confessed.

"Calm down. A guy? Is this a joke?" Tim looked around.

"No. Don't make me regret trusting you," Lucas warned.

"Sorry, okay. You faked being into blonde women pretty well," Tim said.

"I played to a stereotype. I didn't *not* like them. I just never... It doesn't matter. Jack is pissed. I think he broke some rule about being with a patient. I don't know what to do." Lucas stared at the menu, despite knowing exactly what he'd get.

"Don't panic. You can change therapists for the last few weeks or get released. You're moving good. Do the exercises at home. Jack can help but it's not official." Tim wagged an eyebrow.

Lucas laughed. "You're not freaking out."

"There were a few times when you got really drunk and who you were staring at didn't line up with the women you'd been flirting with all night. You never hit on them in public or anything but it made me wonder," Tim admitted.

"Did I ever?" Lucas was afraid to ask.

"No, you never hit on me. Should I be insulted?" Tim asked.

"Guess you're not my type. You're not hiding anything?" Lucas asked.

Tim snickered. "No, I do like women. I've been spoiled in your wake. It's okay."

"I know. I mean, I'm sorry. I wasn't sure. I didn't know. Jack is the first." Lucas scrubbed his hands over his face. "I'm going to blow up my life."

Tim scoffed. "Please, your mom will be thrilled. No daughter-in-law to challenge her cooking talent or decorating taste. She'll have another son, which she loves. Oh God, if you adopt a little girl, Mama Burr will have her in every pageant from baby dolls to Miss Texas."

"Kids, whoa. Stop," Lucas said.

"You always said you were waiting for the right lady and you wanted the traditional family life. Good old Texas spread and a bunch of kids. Was that all lies?" Tim asked.

"I don't know what I want. I need Jack." Lucas felt lost.

"You'll work it out. It's a blip," Tim pointed out.

The waitress arrived and they placed their order. Lucas skipped any alcohol.

"Greg will freak a bit. The rodeo fans will have to adjust but so what? If you're happy…you always loved ranching more," Tim said.

"Thanks, that's why I wanted to meet with you. I need advice from someone who isn't my family, who doesn't make money off me and who I haven't slept with. I feel like I owe the rodeo and fans so much," Lucas said.

Tim nodded. "People just want to see you. They keep asking if you're okay. If you're out of bed. You not showing up. It feels like there's a hole at least in Burrwood Rodeo. Ride in on a nice tame horse and people will feel better."

"I can start making appearances. Greg is setting up meetings. It just sucks. I want Jack. I want him there with me," Lucas admitted.

"Have you told him that?" Tim asked.

Lucas shook his head. "He's worried about his job. I'm worried I'll chicken out."

Tim drummed his fingers on the table. "Sorry, I think if it was that good, he'll find a way to talk to you…once it doesn't threaten his job. He'd get a reputation for doing extra personalized therapy for his patients and it'll be awful. Ugly. You could turn it around and say he took advantage."

"I know, if I push too much, I'm a jerk. If I don't try, he might think I don't care or will hang him out to dry. It's a no-win situation." Lucas shrugged.

"You left messages so you're trying to communicate in a discreet way. He might just not be ready for that yet or he might want a big display of you outing yourself." Tim paused.

Their food arrived and Lucas took a deep breath. Diving into the food, the men talked football and horses. Romance was far too complicated a topic.

* * * *

Another day without Lucas, when he had an appointment. This didn't look good for him. Jack headed for Ken's office after work to discuss things, and head off rumors or concerns.

Brenda walked out just as Jack was going to knock. Ken looked flustered but Jack charged right in.

"Lucas skipped today. I'm sure it's just various work conflicts. He left a message that he went to see his doctor in Houston so we'll get updated information shortly," Jack explained.

"Good. I'm not worried. Brenda is growing very popular with the residents. She's also working on her financing," Ken said.

"She's the competition. Of course she is." Jack shook his head. "I see your first-choice status is very fleeting."

"I know you thought you had it in the bag but my financing options didn't turn out to be as great as I'd hoped. You buying in for a partnership that's just business, you can't own part of something without risking something. Brenda is all for it and she'd like to have Teddy manage the staff. He'd get a promotion as well. I like that attitude," Ken said.

"She has no people skills and with her being a partner, she'd be able to push Teddy around so she'd get whatever jobs she wants," Jack countered.

"But everyone is happier. Except you. You were the star but now our featured patient is MIA. Whatever the explanation, people not getting the treatment their docs want isn't good for us." Ken shrugged.

Jack nodded. "I understand. Lucas is a rebel, like a lot of rodeo guys or athletes. They think they'll heal faster doing their activity than doing what we say. He's had a few setbacks because of that and I even had to make a house call."

"No, now that isn't your job. We don't bill for that. With the new set-up and location we will, but that's all from the hospital right now," Ken argued.

"It wasn't professional, so there's no bill. It was as a friend but he's dealing with work expectations that aren't normal. He falls off a bull for a living. Getting hurt and living with pain is more normal to him. His work colleagues think he's being a wimp and we're telling him to slow way down. The mixed messages are a problem," he explained.

Ken sighed. "I hear that but if he wants to keep working in the rodeo, he needs to properly heal. Let him get a shrink if he needs that sort of help. Hopefully the doc told him all that and he'll be back here working out like normal. Injuries are part of all sports but the rodeo could probably use more medics, trainers and so forth around."

"I'm not familiar with rodeo procedures," Jack admitted.

"You seem to be keeping Lucas very close with your house calls but avoiding the rodeo scene. Weird." Ken leaned back in his squeaky chair.

"You said to stay out of our patients' personal business unless it's directly relevant and they are okay with it. Patient privacy and all that?" he reminded him.

"If he invites you to the rodeo or you choose to attend one, whether he's there or not, that's not a privacy violation. It's a public event. You and I both know we'd love the business," he said.

"I'll see what I can do." Jack forced a smile. "See you tomorrow."

He left and texted his cousin on the way out the door. He needed a night out that involved drinking.

"Jack." Teddy caught him as he nearly got to his car.

"Teddy, I'm on my way to plans with the cousins, sorry," Jack said.

"Okay, well, tomorrow. I'm setting you up with Mark—you're in need of fun, and not cousin or platonic fun," Teddy called.

Mark was a nice guy but the last thing Jack wanted to think about. He'd just be a rebound from Lucas now. That wasn't fair.

* * * *

Josie and Dot were sitting in a booth as Jack rolled up. He immediately saw Lucas' truck. What were the odds? He'd made plans outside of town to avoid him.

No way was he making his cousins go somewhere else just to avoid Lucas. Jack headed right in and settled into their booth. No doubt Lucas had found some VIP section.

"You okay?" Dot asked.

"Yeah, just work." Jack sat and flipped through the menu.

The waitress strolled up and they ordered quickly.

"Sure you don't want a drink?" Josie asked.

"Maybe later. Just iced tea for now. I don't know how one person can throw your life into chaos," Jack confessed.

Dot nodded.

Jack looked at Josie. "You told her?"

"We're sisters. No secrets. But things look worse," Josie said.

"I only told Josie because she's in medicine. She gets the rules about patients," he explained to Dot.

She waved it off. "Got it. What's going on?" she asked.

"Lucas is skipping appointments. It got weird and then there's a change in the business potentially coming. I might have a chance to buy into the business or get a promotion but everyone is after a positive move," he explained.

"Bad timing for that to hit together. But you can do this," Dot said.

"Do what?" Jack asked.

"Whatever you want. Guys come and go, but a good one is worth negotiating with. No one is perfect," Dot replied.

"And the boss?" Jack asked.

"A good one of those is nearly impossible to find, but Ken's a jerk anyway. You know the hospital would hire you." Josie sounded so positive.

"Not my first choice but a job," Jack agreed.

"You could just talk to Lucas and smooth it all over," Josie said.

"It won't smooth anything over. He's left me a few messages, but he doesn't get it. I guess no one is trying to blackmail him." Jack sipped his tea.

"Blackmail?" Dot asked.

Josie frowned. "This is news."

"I know—it's probably just a joke or fishing for info. Someone called and said they had photos of Lucas and me kissing and something else. It's out of context—probably out of focus. They're threatening to publish them if I don't give them a story and an exclusive statement or something." Jack shook his head. "I said no, of course."

"Is it true? You two are a thing?" Dot asked.

"Not really. I can't do that with a patient. You know that. I put a stop to it, but it's all my fault anyway." Jack put a finger to his lips as the waitress brought their food.

Jack had gone with good old comfort food, chicken tenders and fries, but even that wasn't tempting his appetite.

"Okay, so you like him?" Dot asked.

Jack lifted a shoulder. "I'm not the sort of guy he dates. I think it's just a patient-caretaker thing. Or he's experimenting. Either way it could get me fired, in deep crap and he just goes back to rodeo groupies."

"Rodeo groupies? I didn't see any," Lucas said mockingly as he strolled up to their booth.

"How did your photo shoot go?" Jack didn't let Lucas fluster him.

"Good, pictures." Lucas shrugged. "Tim Haynes, old rodeo pal, Jack Gable my physical therapist and..."

"My cousins, Dot and Josie." Jack filled in the gap in introductions.

"A pleasure." Lucas tipped his hat.

"What a coincidence," Dot said.

"We don't want to interrupt your dinner," Lucas said.

"You can join for a drink," Josie suggested.

"Actually, I was going to nag Tim onto the mechanical bull. The restaurant has one in the back. Any interest in watching him?" Lucas asked.

"Our food just arrived," Dot replied.

"Maybe I should try?" Jack asked.

"You? You want to try it?" Lucas asked.

"He did it plenty before, in college. For fun." Josie smiled.

"I'd like to see that," Lucas teased.

"You're not going to ride yet?" Jack asked.

"No, I promise. My doctor did clear me to ride tame horses, though," Lucas said.

"Good for you. I saw you went to the doctor and blew off your PT appointment." Jack slid from the booth.

He ignored the tension and headed for the back room.

Tim went first. He stayed on for a while and drew a crowd. The time he hit gave them a free dinner. Jack wanted to beat his friend but doubted he'd do it. Only because the longer that bull ran, the more force it jerked its rider around with. Tim was physically used to that. Jack would let go before anything close to an injury happened. He wasn't eighteen anymore.

When they asked who was next, Jack went right up to the mechanical bull and the employee helped him up. Lucas dished out the fee and Jack settled in.

"Keep your body loose, only your hand grip and thighs tight," the employee advised.

Jack closed his eyes. Cutting out the visual let his listen to his body and move with the bull. The big cushions rather than hard ground made it much easier to stay relaxed as well. There was no chance of being flung into a fence or guardrail like a real rodeo.

The bull started, slow at first. His cousins cheered and Jack smiled. Relaxing his joints every time they tensed, he rocked with the bull. The more force, the more he tried to correct himself and felt the jerking of the bull. The faster it moved, the more he instinctively opened his eyes to orient himself but it didn't help. He found himself looking for Lucas then his vision blurred from the motion.

"You're doing so good!" Josie yelled.

"Go, Jack!" Lucas shouted.

He opened his eyes and tried to find Lucas again. The emotional distraction and a quick turn of the bull sent Jack flying. The crowd cheered. For a second, he understood why Lucas and Tim liked it. But despite the cushions that broke his fall, Jack was still aching from head to toe.

Lucas helped him up.

"You okay?" he asked.

"You distracted me," Jack said.

"Sorry. Cheering crowds come with the ride." He smacked Jack's arm playfully and held on to him a bit too long.

Dot and Josie shared a look.

"Sorry, habit. Rodeo thing," Lucas said.

"Yeah, sure. Come on, Lucas," Tim said.

"No, I need to talk to Jack," Lucas insisted.

An employee came over and handed Jack a coupon for a free appetizer.

"We better get back to our food," Jack said.

The employee smiled. "We'll have the kitchen warm it up for you. Spontaneous bull riding happens here."

"Thanks," Jack said.

He and his cousins went toward the tables. Lucas and Tim headed for the door.

When he slid back into the booth, he noticed a receipt on the table. A note was scribbled on the ticket. "Paid in full by Lucas Burr. Dessert and tip included."

"That man always has to have the last word." Jack crumpled the receipt.

Dot and Josie shared a look.

"What?" Jack asked.

"Nothing," Dot replied.

"If the last word is dessert, I'm okay with this guy," Josie teased.

"Chocolate is definitely in order, and alcohol," Dot advised.

Jack sighed. If he couldn't have Lucas, he'd have a lot of chocolate tonight and alcohol. Riding the bull wasn't nearly as satisfying as riding a bull rider.

# Chapter Fourteen

The next night, Lucas found himself dragged out to a fancy dinner with Greg, Mama and Tim.

"Why are you sulking?" Mama asked.

"I'm not. I'm pissed off. I said ride in on a tame horse, not ride a bull in the biggest rodeo in Texas as a headliner," he said.

Greg shook his head. "You said you wanted the best deal we could get. To show you were still in the game. This puts you right back on top."

"I'll take it if you don't want it," Tim offered.

Lucas nodded. "He goes on after me."

Greg sighed. "The deal is done."

"It's not done until I show up. Add something on," Lucas replied.

"You got hurt, you don't have the advantage," Greg pointed out.

"They want him, he does have all the leverage," Mama countered.

Tim leaned forward. "I was joking. You don't have to make it a thing."

"Why not? Might get me out of it," Lucas said. "Greg, you don't make deals without talking to me."

"We were always on the same page, kid. Since when are you always zagging when you should zig?" Greg asked.

"Don't call him *kid*. He's a grown man," Mama fussed.

"If you want out, get out. This game crap is only hurting your chances," Tim said to Lucas.

"Chances of what?" Greg butted his nose in.

"Nothing." Lucas checked his phone. "I answered some of those questions in that feature the way I always do but it came off wrong."

"What do you mean? Everyone loves the article. You on your ranch, on a bull you own and back in the saddle." Mama beamed with pride.

"I know, but I'm pushing it. The doc didn't clear me for rodeo riding," Lucas reminded them.

"That's why it's not for a few weeks. We negotiated that so you have time to get stronger. We have time to hype it. Plus, you can ride a tame horse in the home parade first if you want. It looks better tipping your hat to your hometown and then showing off in a big city," Greg explained.

"I agree. Hometown first but a tame ride." Mama sipped her champagne. "It's a shame your brothers won't be back in time."

Lucas chuckled. His brothers stayed away. Now he understood why Jack seemed content away from his parents. Sometimes the direct pressure of a core family could be suffocating.

"Seriously, Lucas. You seem depressed. You're improving. You'll be on top in no time. Don't let that doctor or those physical therapy people get you down because they want you to be careful. Your business isn't playing safe but you know how to do it safely." Mama really believed every word.

It made no sense but he'd reassured her so many times that she swallowed it. She only fretted when he was in actual pain.

"Maybe you should have a drink," Greg suggested.

Lucas shook his head. "I'm fine. I'm glad the opportunities are there but rushing to ride could backfire. Luck runs out for everyone."

"You're thinking about your dad. Honey, only God knows when any of our times is up. You got a scare with that fall but you have to put that behind you and do what you love. We're all here supporting you because we know you love it and we want you to be happy." Mama patted his arm.

"I know, but you said it was okay if I wanted to stop. You wouldn't feel better if I quit?" Lucas asked.

Greg cleared his throat. "Lucas, don't put your mama in that position."

Mama held up her hand. "I did say all of that. Because I will always support you. And because you could have an injury that you might not be able to recover from one day. Or an injury that won't allow you to ride even if you have relatively normal rest of your life. This is *not* that injury. You just need your confidence back. The sooner you get back on the bull with that timer going and the crowd cheering, the sooner you'll forget all this anxiety. Now, it's all you're thinking about because you're limited."

Nodding, Lucas saw the logic in it. He wasn't practicing or doing his normal routine. Now he was just stewing on the pain and the injury or doing his physical therapy. The mistake in the landing that he probably could've have corrected if he'd felt it sooner. Then again, there were still two suspects out there to talk to.

"Your mama is right. You're all tense and worried. Once you're in that shoot and on that bull, you'll feel like your old self. Living in the moment. It's what you were born for. Your brothers find thrills in other ways. You're a true Texan," Greg said.

Lucas looked at Tim who nodded and shrugged. "You always feel twitchy when you're not riding. Injuries are rough but the longer you're not riding, the harder it is. You'll be fine but I'm all for waiting until the doc clears you."

"He's got time to go back to the doc before the Dallas thing. It's easy to make an appointment for the day before and do all the exercise and PT work you can until then. Think positive," Greg advised. "You've got the prime spot, Lucas. But if you want to give it up to Tim, that's your choice."

"His body might just need more time to heal," Mama corrected.

"Get Tim a spot too and I'll play it your way and we'll see how it goes," Lucas said.

"I'll do my best. Now, shall we call it a night or does anyone want dessert?" Greg asked.

"No, I should get home. I have to walk Baby," Mama said.

"I'm going to go for a drive, clear my head," Lucas said.

Tim stood and shook hands with the men. "Thanks for dinner, Greg. Mrs. Burr." He tipped his hat.

"Good night, Tim." Mama smiled. "He's got good manners. Good friends like that are a help. Every setback isn't a sign or a defeat. Sometimes it's just a little test."

"Thanks, Ma. Thanks for dinner, Greg." Lucas walked away from the table. Walk or drive, he needed to be alone. He missed Jack. He'd have made tonight tolerable but probably would've argued with Greg half the night.

Why did that make Lucas smile so much?

He couldn't be alone with his thoughts. He needed to follow up on the suspects. It was a good excuse to get Jack around again.

Lucas: *Hey Jack, was planning on trying to rattle the investor for info. Want to join? Your ink will make him furious.*

Jack: *How flattering. R u sure u want me along?*

Lucas: *absolutely. Want to really rattle him. pick u up?*

Jack: *k…ready in half an hour…*

Lucas almost felt lightheaded. The rush of knowing he'd get to be with Jack. PT appointments meant other people and being professional. Lucas couldn't do that now.

* * * *

"I'm sorry I've been missing things." Lucas drove. Jack looked great but the tension remained.

"Regrets, it's fine," Jack said.

"I don't regret a thing, except maybe hurting your career if people found out. I've been quiet. I wanted to tell my mom and Greg at dinner the other night but I couldn't," he said.

"But you told Tim," Jack added.

"How did you know?" Lucas asked.

Jack sighed. "The way he looked at me with the whole mechanical bull situation. My cousins know."

"Okay, so they hate me," Lucas said.

"They don't understand. I don't either. If you like sleeping with men more, why don't you?" Jack asked.

"Come on," Lucas said.

"It'll ruin your career, potentially anyway. Let's talk about this investor." Jack changed the subject.

"Mr. Dewitt. Devout Christian with some strong and ugly right leanings. I vetoed him. I didn't think he'd agree to talk to me, but he did." Lucas took the turn off onto the guy's spread.

"He doesn't know I'm coming?" Jack asked.

Lucas shook his head. "No, I needed backup."

"Tim's not good enough?" Jack asked.

Lucas laughed. "Tim is like a brother. You're nothing like that." He reached over and squeezed Jack's knee.

"Don't." Jack pushed his hands away. "I'm not interested in on-again-off-again games."

"You're right. Let's get this talk over with then we do have things to discuss." Lucas unbuckled his seatbelt.

Jack hung back and followed along. This house look liked a grand mansion out of *Gone with the Wind* complete with a veranda.

Mr. Dewitt was lounging and looking at the sky. "Boys, how nice to see you." He stood and shook hands.

"Thanks. This is Jack. He's helping me recover from the fall," Lucas introduced.

Dewitt tipped his hat. "Nasty fall. Shame."

"It was. We've been wondering if anyone tampered with the ropes or the animal," Jack explained.

"Why would be asking me? I don't go to that rodeo anymore. I wasn't welcome." Dewitt eased back into his recliner.

"That's not true, sir. You're welcome but your friends who wear sheets and use rope for other things than riding, they're not," Lucas explained.

"You're even more of a liberal than your father." Dewitt studied the ink on Jack's arm. "Gay company too."

"Watch it," Jack said.

"No offense. Live and let live—until you burn," he replied. "Oh, I get it. You think it was me because I didn't get to invest in your rodeo. No, I don't do vengeance. That's for the Lord."

"You don't get a spread like this without putting your enemies in their place," Jack replied.

Dewitt grinned. "I like you. The only revenge I'm ever after is success. I bought a bit of land between here and Dallas. A big stretch. Working on the zoning but in a few weeks, we break ground on the Biggest Christian Rodeo and Amusement Park in Texas. Nothing but clean and wholesome fun for the whole family. Rides for all ages, issues and abilities. Plus, food, restaurants and rodeo. Petting zoo and pictures with the animals. Every inch of the place a clean safe space for you to take your grandma or your baby girl. That is a recipe for success. I'm thinking of opening more along the Bible belt. High standards, low prices."

"Closed on Sundays?" Jack joked.

"No, that's a day to rest, put God and family first all for half price. We'd have services ongoing all day long starting on the hour. You and your family could hit a worship service, then share a meal, and enjoy the day as a family. And think of the jobs for good people—from cooks to mechanics. I'll need them all," he said.

"You do dream big, Dewitt. Congrats," Lucas said.

Dewitt shook Lucas' hand again. "I'm sorry if someone did try to hurt you or the bull. But it wasn't me and you should let the Lord sort that out."

Lucas nodded. "I'm not looking for revenge. If it's personal I can let it go. If it's someone just out to hurt animals or riders, I can't let that go on. As an owner I'm responsible for my riders. It might not be me next time. Then I'm not protecting my riders or the animals."

"That is a predicament. I'm going to pray for you. Both of you. Good-looking fella like you, Jack, you could have all the ladies after you. I'd be happy to pay to get that tattoo removed whenever you see the light," Dewitt offered.

"I'm good, thanks," Jack replied.

"Nice meeting you." Dewitt extended his hand.

Jack felt very odd. "You sure you want to shake my hand again?"

"We're all sinners. No one is perfect. I think Lucas brought you here for a reason."

Jack smiled. He felt the same way but he doubted it was whatever Dewitt had in mind.

"Good luck with the amusement park. You know banning people like me is illegal, right? Even on private property," Jack said.

Dewitt sighed. "What happened to people's rights? Personal freedom is under attack. But who else other than Christians would show up? If I have to let in some heathens, maybe they'll see the light. Just to prove it, I'll make sure you boys get VIP tickets for opening weekend. Bring your lady friends."

"Very kind, Mr. Dewitt," Lucas said.

"And if I bring my boyfriend?" Jack pushed.

"We might just assume he's your brother but if you two cross any lines, we'll have to ask you to leave," Dewitt admitted.

Jack stepped in closer. "If Lucas kissed his girlfriend in the park. That's okay?"

Dewitt smiled. "Sure."

"But if I kissed a guy, that's a problem?" Jack asked.

"A big one. I don't want to see that any more than my patrons will," he replied.

"I'm sorry to hear that." Jack grabbed Lucas and kissed him hard.

Jack expected Lucas to pull away or punch him but Lucas pulled Jack in closer and returned the kiss.

Both men froze at the sound of a gun cocking.

They looked over and Dewitt had a pistol pointed at them. "You two go now and never come back on my land."

"No problem," Jack said.

Lucas took a step toward Dewitt and punched him square in the face.

"Lucas!" Jack grabbed his hand and pulled him to the truck.

Jack got behind the wheel and drove back to his place.

"What did I just do?" Lucas asked.

"I'm not entirely sure," Jack admitted.

* * * *

In Jack's apartment, he got an ice pack for Lucas' hand. Roscoe licked Lucas' face.

"I love that you punched him," Jack said.

"Why did you kiss me?" Lucas asked.

"I had to. The guy was playing all nicey-nice but if I was black or Asian, he'd have turned the gun on me immediately. If he hadn't seen the ink, he'd have assumed I was straight and probably said a lot more offensive things."

"Now he knows," Lucas said.

"Yeah, sorry but you did kiss me back pretty good. So?" Jack asked.

Lucas shook his head. "I thought I got to decide if I ever outed myself."

Jack sighed. "It was one guy who is a religious nutjob. We both deny it, no one will believe him."

"He probably has a million security cameras on his land," Lucas argued.

"I didn't think about that. I didn't think. I just wanted to rub his face in it. You could've shoved me away. I want us." Jack's phone pinged.

"Probably pictures of us all over the Internet," Lucas said.

"No, Lexi from work saying your interview is up. I guess I missed it." Jack opened the file.

"Don't, you don't have to read it. It's a boring interview," Lucas said.

Jack kept out of Lucas' reach. "You do look hot on that bull. What? Why can't I read it?" Jack scrolled through the questions.

Jack froze when he found it.

"When asked if Lucas had a special lady in his life, he replied that he was still looking for that one and only *cowgirl* to ride off into the sunset with," Jack read.

"That's the same answer I've been giving in interviews since I was a teenager," Lucas explained.

"I understand." Jack gritted his teeth.

"No, you don't. I was in pain. I was thrilled about our night but overwhelmed." Lucas moved closer.

Jack backed away. "Yeah? I'm fine. It's fine. My job was to make you feel better. Apparently, I really went above and beyond. I got star struck or something. But my job is over."

"No, we have a session in the morning. You can move me to someone else but that might look suspicious," Lucas said.

Jack wanted to tell him about the blackmail call. But they hadn't published anything. It might've been an idle threat and telling Lucas would just hurt him. It'd be revenge or punishment—a threat of what might happen. This wasn't Jack's area of expertise.

He decided to sleep on it. "I'll see you in the morning for your session. I'm tired. Good night."

"Jack, no. I don't want to go," Lucas said.

"What if Dewitt hires a PI to watch you? Bring back proof that you are…that we are something more than friends? He says he's not into revenge but he might see it as a good deed, pushing us to covert to women," Jack mocked.

Lucas sighed. "I'll go because you don't seem yourself and I don't want to upset you more. I told Tim. I'll tell my mom and Greg soon."

"It's your secret to tell. I'm nothing in your story," Jack said.

# Chapter Fifteen

The tension in the private room was more than Lucas could handle. He pulled away every time Jack touched him.

"What?" Jack asked.

"We're alone—you could relax a bit or tell me what's bothering you," Lucas said.

"All business at the PT office. We agreed. You're not the only one with problems," Jack replied.

"Is it Dewitt? I punched him because he was rude to you. I'm used to those guys. I heard what my dad always told me as a kid but meant something different now," Lucas said.

"What did your dad say?" Jack asked.

*"Don't cry. Be tough. Be a real cowboy."* Lucas closed his eyes.

"Guys can cry and be tough. You're the realest cowboy I've ever met. Rescuing their boyfriends from bigoted old creeps." Jack leaned.

"Boyfriend?" Lucas' mouth went dry for a minute and he grabbed his water.

"Sorry." The gleam went out of Jack's eye.

"It's fine. You're right, we're at your office right now. I don't want any trouble for you. We should focus on the case. Dewitt didn't call me about blackmail. Did he call you?" Lucas asked.

"No, that guy doesn't need our money," Jack scoffed. "But I think I should tell you something."

"What?" Lucas stood and moved in closer.

"I got a call. It was a gossip site or online newspaper wanting to cover… They say they had proof we kissed. Pics from the mall and pics from you leaving my apartment building the next morning. They tried to get me to give them a story. My side of it or something. I didn't. I hung up and didn't tell them anything," he said.

Lucas' heart jumped in his throat as his gut twisted up. "I'm sorry. I'll deal with them."

"There's nothing to deal with. They tried to bribe me for a story at first. Painting you as a playboy. When that didn't work, they tried to blackmail me. No idea if or when it'll really come out. They haven't so far so odds are good. But I wanted you to know—I didn't give them any info and I didn't take any money. They might be trying to dig up other men you've been with for more dirt. Whatever happens, I kept my mouth shut." Jack opened the door and left.

Lucas wanted to jump off the treadmill and chase Jack down but this was his work. Making a scene here would only piss him off more.

Lucas had thought they'd gotten away with a bit of privacy. Of course, they'd get photos of the one guy he'd ever dated. He grabbed his phone and texted Greg about the potential gossip story. It didn't matter what was true or not—they just needed to have a response ready.

Now he realized why he'd been driving himself crazy. Jack deserved better than to deal with celebrity crap and having people all over him all the time. Lucas had agreed to it, he understood it was part of the business, but Jack hadn't signed up for it. He'd tried to wait and keep things professional. It wasn't his fault their attraction was so strong.

Lucas finished his treadmill time with extra rage and adrenaline. Finally, he was done and he left without a word to anyone. This wasn't the time or place for it anyway. Jack seemed done with him. If only it was that easy to evict Jack from his heart.

* * * *

After almost no sleep, Jack dragged himself out of bed and into the shower. It barely helped but coffee did. Lucas was all he could think about. He wanted more—he wanted to fix it. Not that he'd done anything wrong...well, they both had in some ways. In others, he felt for Lucas trying to find himself.

But Jack deserved respect and a life of his own as well. He'd never wanted anything to upset Lucas. The world just wasn't always kind to celebrities with secrets.

Leaving for work, Jack nearly tripped over something. The backsplash of coffee on his scrubs was bad enough. He looked down. He didn't have any papers delivered—only his more senior neighbors did that anymore. Grabbing the paper, he didn't recognize it. Finally, he unrolled it to see the title. The *Texas Tattler*.

He and Lucas were right there kissing on the front page.

Frozen for a moment, he didn't know which way to go. His hands shook but he couldn't let this make him give up. He had to go to work. After locking the door behind him, he went down to his truck and shut himself in there.

He'd never read so fast in his life. Was it making any sense? The story painted Jack as a seductive nurse who'd lured Lucas into the homosexual lifestyle.

"I'm not a nurse," he muttered to himself. Jack shook his head. That was a fact he could prove was wrong but it didn't matter. This was all over the Internet and fighting it—with those pictures, how could he fight it?

His cell phone rang. It was her mother. He ignored the call and started the car. Driving to work, he tried to imagine how it would go. What Teddy would say? Ken?

Shaking it off, he parked his car and got out. He had clients to work with. Thankfully Lucas not on the list for today.

Jack put his lunch in the fridge and filled his water bottle. When Teddy walked in, he wanted to jump off a bridge. The look on his face said it all.

"Jack, I don't know if you saw?" Teddy started.

"I saw and it's crap," he said.

Teddy frowned. "Sure, right. That's what I thought. You two always seemed to fight more than…"

"Teddy, please don't." Jack took a sip of water.

"Okay, sure. But the pics—I know they can Photoshop crap. Denial isn't your style, Jack," Teddy said.

"Whatever it was, it was a momentary mistake. A slip. Over before it started," he said.

Teddy smiled. "You might want to work on that. Sounds like you're trying to convince yourself more than me."

Jack checked the schedule. He was on the nursing home today. Of course. At least maybe they'd ignore that sort of trash and he'd be away from the gossips.

When Brenda walked in, the vibe changed.

"No wonder you wanted Lucas all to yourself." Brenda dropped a copy of the *Tattler* on one of the tables.

"It's trash, Brenda," Teddy said.

"Don't defend him. Pictures are worth a lot and that picture doesn't look doctored. Very hot and heavy with roaming hands," she replied.

"You know a lot about Photoshop, do you?" Teddy asked.

Jack smiled. "You don't have to defend me, Teddy. It's history. Nothing."

"But you did do this." Brenda pointed to the paper.

"It's a real photo," Jack confessed.

Lying would only make this worse. At least Jack could hide over at the nursing home and avoid Ken.

He headed for the door when Ken walked in. "Go home."

"What?" Jack asked.

"I saw the papers. I need to review things. You're not working today," he said.

"What about the nursing home residents?" Jack asked.

"They can have one day off. You called in sick. I'm going to investigate this. Speak with Lucas and your other patients. Make sure there is no other inappropriate behavior on your part," Ken said.

"What? No, it wasn't inappropriate. Lucas, yes, but it's not like what they wrote in that rag. I never got involved with anyone else I worked with or a patient. It wasn't a seduction," he swore.

"Go home. I'll call you," he said.

"What about my side?" Jack demanded.

"Fine, my office. I'm going to need coffee for this," Ken grumbled.

Jack headed for the office, not sure what he was going to say to defend himself.

He sat down and tried to feel bad. It was wrong to do that with a patient but deep down he missed Lucas. Jack wanted more, not less. How could something be wrong and right at the same time?

Ken closed the door behind him then sat down with a grunt. "I knew you'd been acting funny. I thought it was the promotion talk. If Lucas was out of line, you should've come to me. I protect my employees."

"He wasn't out of line," Jack admitted.

"This isn't him grabbing and kissing you?" Ken asked.

Jack shook his head. "I decided a different approach to his therapy might help. I took him hiking and then walking around the mall in the next town. Some people don't do well in the PT rooms. It can add to their depression. I instigated this."

"Okay, that's nothing new but that doesn't make it okay for a patient to think it's a date." Ken flipped open the paper. "Is this him leaving your apartment building? That could be fake," he said.

Jack didn't reply.

"How far did this go?" Ken asked.

"I started it. It was my fault. I kissed him first," Jack replied.

"You slept with a patient?" he asked.

Jack nodded.

"Was this some new form of therapy? Because we don't support that here," Ken said.

"No, it just happened. I kissed him. I tried to stop it and explain why I couldn't. He kissed me and I...it just happened."

"He overpowered you?" Ken asked.

"No, I wanted it. You think Lucas and I have been having issues because he's rushing things. I want him better and I tried to get him to see another therapist. If he'd only agreed to that," Jack said.

"I tried to get him to do that as well when I saw him skipping appointments. He said you're the only one he trusted. He was having personal issues at home that made his schedule unpredictable. I believed him. Now I find out he was taking advantage of you." Ken crumpled the paper up.

"I told you he wasn't. I'm not the victim," he said.

Ken patted his desk. "I understand. I know how they made that story sound but Jack, he's a celebrity. A huge name in this town and major rodeo star. You're out, he knew that. He's hiding his preferences so he used you for his needs. Being star struck and a bit attracted to the guy... People understand. We're medical professionals but we're human. We make mistakes. He became infatuated with a caregiver—it happens as well. You should've drawn a firmer line."

"I'm sorry. I didn't mean for it to happen. It'll never happen again," Jack said.

Ken rubbed his neck. "Thank you. Now, I do want you to go home today. I'll speak with Lucas and see how he wants to proceed with this PR nightmare. I'll be in touch."

"Thanks." Jack left and had no idea what to do with himself.

Going to see Lucas was all he wanted, but keeping a low profile was smarter for everyone.

# Chapter Sixteen

Ever since Jack warned him about the gossip rag trying to get him to contribute to their story, Lucas had been trying to shut it down. Greg had no luck. The rodeo groups had had no luck either.

Lucas wasn't going to talk to them. That was a mistake he'd made before. They'd twist and turn things around to make everyone look dirty or unethical. If they couldn't kill the article, they were screwed. Greg had offered to arrange a bribe to kill it but Lucas didn't trust that they would actually pull the plug on it. They'd just take the money and run then turn it around that he'd tried to stop the free press.

Lucas loved freedom and America but trashing people for being consenting adults? He'd called Jack four times, but Jack was clearly radio silent for now. One last attempt before he went stir crazy… He called the PT office and got Teddy.

"Hey, it's Lucas. Is Jack there?" Lucas asked.

Teddy cleared his throat. "No comment."

"Teddy, I know. I'm the one to blame. It's all my fault. I need to find Jack and talk to him," he said.

"Jack is taking the blame, so you don't have to worry," Teddy replied.

Lucas swore under his breath. "I don't want that. I want him. I know it's a mess but it's my fault. I'm sorry Mark is the odd man out but I couldn't admit it before. Please, help me narrow down where to find Jack. He's not taking my calls."

"He's not here. They sent him home. I can't imagine he's out wandering the town." Teddy hung up.

Lucas stared at his phone. The messages and calls were blowing up but he ignored most of them. That was a risk. Going to Jack's home, there might be some reporters or random losers trying to get pics of them and sell them to the gossip sites. People made money off others misery and create scandal. Lucas took risks with his own life, but playing with other people's lives and reputations was just cruel.

He thought about getting Tim to drive by and see if it was safe but Lucas had no patience. He drove over to Jack's and spied no one lurking in the bushes. Cameras today could photograph from huge distances but were they worth that sort of a lens? That much trouble? It seemed so juvenile.

He jogged up the stairs and knocked on the door.

Not a peep came from the other side.

"Jack, I know you're in there. Please, let's talk," Lucas said.

"I warned you. Just let me take the fall. They'll forget all about it by Dallas," he said.

"The gay horses are way out of the barn on this one. Let me in. I don't want to bother your neighbors," he said.

He needed to see Jack, to see that he was okay.

"Just leave," Jack said.

"I can make a scene—you know I can," he teased.

He tried the door. After a few seconds Jack opened it.

"What?" he asked.

He moved inside and closed the door behind him. Pulling him close, he felt a million times better. "That paper did me a huge favor."

"I don't believe you. It'll going to come crashing down on you. I'm fine," Jack insisted.

"I'm not. I tried to kill that story. Believe me but it's oddly a huge relief." He leaned down and kissed Jack.

For a few sweet moments Jack kissed him back but then the tension returned and he slipped from Lucas' grasp.

"No, that's not going to fix anything now. I can handle my own mess. You being here will only make it worse," he said.

"Why? How? If we're more than a hookup, then no one can say anything. It's just about me being gay," he said.

"Yes, and you are way too calm about that. It'll catch up with you. My job is still in jeopardy. Didn't Ken call you?" he asked.

Lucas nodded. "He did, I told him I flirted and encouraged it all. I made the first moves, which is the truth. But it was real, not some caregiver crap. You know that's not it."

"You still need PT. Brenda or Teddy will take care of you." Jack sat on the couch and clutched a decorative pillow.

"I don't want them. I trust you. I need you." He knelt next to him.

"No, you don't. You'll be ready for Dallas or you won't. I can't stop you. You don't listen to me. You just do what you want or get the doc to sign off on it. I'm sure you'll do the same thing. I'm sorry I wasted your time trying to get you to do things my way," he said.

"You didn't. You're great. I'm not hiding anymore. I can't. The pictures, the truth…it's done. I don't blame you for that." The hurt look in Jack's eyes made Lucas want to go back and change everything if he could. Jack's fight seemed to be gone. He didn't believe that Lucas would follow through with coming out? Would he make it a joke? Blame Jack? Blame the misinformed media?

"You might blame me when your career blows up. Your family will blame me. But that's not the problem. I'm in love with you," Jack said.

Lucas took a deep breath. "I think I am too but it's scary. We don't have to rush into anything."

"You don't understand." Jack shook his head. "I can't…I can't live with the idea of you risking your life every night. I can't watch and cheer for you to nearly break your neck."

Lucas nodded. "Oh."

"We never talked about that. We never talked about a real relationship. If this is real, there's a lot to sort through but that…I just don't think I could get used to it. I can't be okay with it."

"Jack, I can't walk away from my career just like that. I can't. I have too much riding on it. I will do everything I can to be ready. You can help." He took his hand.

Jack pulled back. "It's my fault you got sprung from the closet before you were ready. That's wrong. I feel bad enough about that. I should've kept things quieter. Because I can't watch you almost die every night."

"You never mentioned this," Lucas said.

Jack chuckled uneasily. "I never let myself think about it. I never thought I'd get you into bed. Then it got complicates with all of your press interest."

"We should slow down and date. Unless you'd prefer Mark," Lucas joked.

Jack kissed Lucas. "I'd prefer you having a job that's safe. It's just so hard when I know everything that could go wrong."

"I get it but let's not go to an extreme," he said.

"Say you won't ride rodeo for a few months," Jack challenged.

He sighed. "I can't. I have to honor my commitments."

"I get it. You're the star and everyone is counting on you. Some days I'm really glad I left Dallas. My parents were very high pressure and used their money to get their way. I wanted to earn my promotions and stuff on my own. I came here for my uncle but I stayed for me. Your family, friends and fans are encamped around you—it must be suffocating," Jack said.

He nodded. "You do get it. Be there, cheer me on and we'll show them."

Jack shook his head. "I won't watch you fall. And I know you will fall off eventually. You could be hurt. I can't. I can't watch that."

Jack's phone rang. He reached for it. "Hi, Ken."

Lucas held his breath, trying to figure out what to say to help Jack and hoping he wasn't fired on top of everything else. The feeling of helplessness made him angry. What sort of man couldn't protect the man he loved and his family?

"I understand. Yeah, I'll do that." Jack ended the call.

"Bad news?" Lucas asked.

"I'm fired. I can pick up my stuff tomorrow. Not much stuff there anyway," Jack said.

"I'm sorry. I told him it was all me." Lucas sat next to Jack on the couch. "But now we don't have a problem."

"What?" He looked at him with disgust.

"No conflict of interest," he said.

"Are you insane? I don't have a job. I am a laughingstock in this town. A slut screwing my patients. Do you really think us dating is going to fix any of this?" Jack asked.

Lucas wanted to tell Jack to calm down but that seemed like it would backfire. "Yes, if we're seen dating then it's not a one-time thing. It's not that Nightingale thing. It's real. Because it is real, Jack. I love you."

He sighed. "If you really did, you'd respect my knowledge. You'd trust my experience. But you think you know better and want to keep risking your life. Or Greg knows better or someone else but not me. Instead of waiting and seeing how you heal, you bound ahead for your career committing to things. I don't tell you how to ride a bull or break a horse but I know what the future holds for your back."

"I'm sorry. That's not how I meant it to come off. Greg pushed for the best deal and we had to put a date on it. I can back out," he said.

"That's another lie. You'll do it because you're a man of your word. I'm glad if you can rodeo again and if it makes you happy. But I can't be with you. I'd be terrified every time you rode. I will anyway but I can at least start putting distance between us. I have to protect myself even if I can't protect you." He let go of the pillow and turned to him. Jack kissed him. "Please go."

"Jack, no," he said.

"Go, and don't come back," he said.

"What are you going to do?" he asked.

"Maybe I do need to go back to Dallas. Face my family now that I'm stronger. By the time I move back, the story will have died down. I'll get a job and can be anonymous there. That's the good thing about a big city," Jack replied.

"The only good thing," he said.

"It's something. I'll miss my friends and cousins but no one will hire me here." Jack folded his arms.

"I would," Lucas teased.

"That won't do either of us any good. Hiring me…now I'm a hooker." Jack laughed. "Please."

Lucas watched him stand up and make it to the door.

"Go," Jack said.

There was nothing he could do and Jack wouldn't let him just stay. He walked up to him. "I could stay here with you, all night. Make you feel better."

Jack smiled. "Please go."

He kissed Jack slowly. "Call me if you need anything. Call Greg or Mama if you can't get me."

Jack laughed. "Your mom. There is a right way to date and a wrong way. We did everything wrong. This wasn't real. It was all in my head."

"No, it was real. You're choosing to end it. We might not have started off like a fairytale but those aren't real. This is life. Messy, dirty, throw you out of the saddle but you get back up—life in Texas. You're letting them throw you and choosing to stay down." He headed for the door and paused.

Jack sighed. "I'm drawing a line about how much pain I'm willing to take. Not everyone loves the thrill and the fall. I'm sorry, I never thought about this before. We had issues with my work and you being in the closet. Thinking about what you do and living with it…if I loved you less, I might be able to live with it."

Lucas had no words. He opened the door and exited. Leaning on the frame for a moment, he hoped Jack would open the door and drag him back inside. But that was the movie crap again. Jack was hurt and confused. Losing his job, Lucas knew what that did to a man. What Jack needed was time to heal and figure out if he felt Lucas was worth the fight. Lucas had to prove it somehow.

Being away from Jack hurt Lucas just as much, but he couldn't walk away from his whole life.

* * * *

Jack drove to work and cleared out his locker, hoping to be gone before anyone arrived. Falling for Lucas had thrown Jack's life into chaos. Now he had no job and no boyfriend. Lucas had devoted his life to rodeo and asking him to stop wasn't fair. But it was honest. If Lucas didn't care how it made Jack feel—it wouldn't work out.

Hell, Jack never thought Lucas would come out and not freak. No doubt he'd be pissed off now, that he was outed and had lost the guy. Jack had never thought they'd get that far. He'd watched enough footage of Lucas' rides to know how he'd react.

Jack checked the office area to be sure he had all his belongings. Before he'd been the one who opened and closed if Ken was late so he had a set of keys. Ken would probably change the locks now.

Putting the keys on Ken's desk, Jack spotted a tablet. His login might work or it might not, but he had to check. Logging in, Jack went right to Lucas' file. Ken had reassigned Lucas to Brenda. Of course he had. Flipping to the new notes, Jack wanted to throw the tablet into the trash.

*Brenda: Cleared patient Burr to return to normal activity.*

"She can't be serious," Jack said.

"Sneaking in to steal files or clients?" Brenda asked.

"No, I was just getting my stuff and dropping off my keys. You released Lucas to work? Have you even seen him for a session?" Jack asked.

"His doctor released him to ride a horse. Rodeo is a special skill. He has to make that determination," Brenda replied.

"He'll get hurt again," Jack argued.

"Considering the whole sport is trying to stay on an animal trying to throw you off, and ends in everyone getting thrown—yes, I'm sure he'll get hurt again. That's like telling a hockey player to not get body slammed or a football player not to get tackled. They have to make the decision when they want to take that chance again," Brenda agreed.

"You can't be serious," Jack said.

"His doctor has the final say but I'm not blocking a man from making a living. Hopefully we'll have a few more sessions before but patients respond to positive incentives, Jack. Not just sex," Brenda said.

"I can't ever believe I thought you were a friend," Jack said.

Brenda shrugged. "I don't really do friends with co-workers. They all stab you in the back. This time I got you before you got me. Teddy, he's a bit more friendly so he's not a threat."

"A threat to what?" Jack shook his head. "I'm going. With just my stuff. The keys are there."

"Thanks for making my promotion and everything so easy. Good luck," Brenda called.

Jack drove around for a bit. He wanted to think of Brenda as a mean girl but she wasn't even that mean. Just an opportunist who put herself first. To a degree, Jack felt sorry for Brenda. She'd never had a real friend.

Something made Jack drive out to the ranch but he didn't see Lucas' truck. Maybe he was at the rodeo? He couldn't face another fight with him.

Jack's phone rang. Part of him hoped it was Lucas. It was Dot.

"Hi," Jack answered.

"Dad is going to kill that guy," Dot said.

"No, I talked to Aunt Teensy last night. She's got a handle on the situation. I kissed Lucas. You and Josie encouraged me," Jack pointed out.

"Trash papers snooping and blaming you," Dot complained.

"It's worse. I got fired. Lucas and I are done. I can't." The tears welled up so he threw the car in drive and headed for home. The car immediately took the call to the handsfree system so Jack had both hands on the wheel.

"I'll meet you at your place," Dot said.

"Don't you have to work?" Jack asked.

"It's one of those government holidays none of you normal people get off and always forget about. Schools closed and I'm coming over with whiskey."

Two hours later, Jack had resisted day drinking.

"What's the plan?" Dot asked.

Jack shrugged. "Pray he doesn't get hurt."

They'd been talking about Lucas for a couple hours.

"I meant your job. You said Ken was going to start something else?" she asked.

Jack nodded. "Sort of. Maybe. He needed money and was sniffing around for that."

"Why don't you start up a place?" Dot suggested.

"More pressure. I'm single, and let's start a business all by myself with a tarnished reputation and in a small town where the need might not grow fast enough." Jack laughed.

"You are the best physical therapist and everyone knows it. Fine, you don't want that. Do you want to work at the hospital or move back to Dallas? Those are your options," Dot said.

"I still have a big chunk of my college fund left. My dad really wanted me to be a doctor," Jack said.

Dot smiled. "I wanted to work for NASA but life takes us in weird directions. If you have the money, make a business plan, get some business loans, find a building and so on. One of my friends is in real estate."

"One step at a time. I need to figure out if I have enough," Jack said.

"You know Josie and everyone will send people to you. They like you. Brenda is a bitch. Ken is a jerk who never does any work. Teddy, you should steal Teddy away now," Dot said.

"That's premature," Jack said.

"Make a meeting with the bank and see how much you can get. Gotta start somewhere," Dot said.

"I can't think about it. Maybe I should go back to Dallas. Then I'll avoid Lucas." Jack's stomach knotted up at the idea of not seeing him again.

"You really love him." Dot groaned. "You need to stay and figure it out."

"Could you be with a guy who routinely gets on a bull only to be thrown off? You know he's going to hit the ground and that animal might trample him," Jack explained.

Dot shrugged. "I don't know. I don't love him. But you were in the military. You took risks."

Jack smiled. "Exactly. I saw friends die and their widows and kids crying. I couldn't get in a relationship when I was deployed. I just couldn't. This might be a bit less dangerous but the risk is real."

Dot scrunched up her nose. "We should go to the rodeo."

"His big ride in Dallas? I don't think I can do that," Jack admitted.

"You won't be alone. We'll all be there. I'll call your dad and he'll get us good tickets. We're family, we stick together." Dot pulled out her phone.

Jack didn't stop his cousin. It terrified him but Jack wasn't ready to let go of Lucas yet. If he was hurt on his first ride back, Jack needed to be there. Not as an EMT or PT specialist—as someone who loves him.

"No argument?" Dot asked.

Jack shook his head. "I'll call the bank tomorrow and set up a meeting."

Dot hugged Jack. "Good for you."

* * * *

After calling the bank and tucking Dot in on the sofa to sleep off her day-drinking, Jack made a few more calls about one Donnie Smith.

Even if Jack couldn't have Lucas, he could make sure he was safe going forward. When Jack drove there, he felt it was oddly familiar. It was the very same ranch where they had inspected the bull.

A hand walked up to Jack when he got out of the truck.

"Can I help?" the guy asked.

"I'm looking for Donnie Smith," Jack said.

"He's in the big barn there, feeding the horses. Looking for work? We ain't got any openings," the guy added.

"No, I just need a quick word with Donnie. About an old mutual friend," Jack said. In the barn, he watched for humans in the stalls full of horses. A barn cat peeked out and hissed at him.

Then a man leaned out of one of the stalls.

"You lost?" he asked.

"Looking for Donnie Smith." Jack walked closer.

"You found him. Unless he owes you money," the guy joked.

"Nah, I just wondered… I'm Jack Gable by the way." The men shook hands. "I heard you used to work for Burr ranch. They don't seem to lose a lot of hands. What happened?"

"What business is it of yours?" Donnie asked.

"None, but I wondered if the Burrs were good to work for. If they were unfair in anyway?" Jack asked.

Donnie brushed the horse and shook his head. "No, not really. They're good folks. Pay decent and are honest. But they're tough."

"Tough, meaning?" Jack prompted.

"You don't look like a ranch hand," Donnie said.

"I know they fired you for stealing. Was it true?" Jack asked.

Donnie looked around. "True and right aren't the same things."

Jack folded his arms. "You did steal?"

"Not for myself." Donnie shook his head.

"I need more than that." Jack tried to see the best in people but he wasn't going to be played.

"Why should I trust you? Are you trying to get me fired? It took a long time and a lie detector test to get this job. This is a job illegal people can get," Donnie said in a panic.

"Like the other ranch hand who was fired for stealing. He's in ICE custody now. Did it bother you that you got paid the same as someone without documents? You stole to make it even or something?" Jack asked.

"No, I'm not like that. His family didn't have any papers. Some of them had trouble finding work. I helped him steal to keep them afloat. The Burrs could afford it," Donnie said.

"Did he try asking for help instead of just stealing? Asking if they needed more help or something?" Jack asked.

"He was proud. Didn't even want to take my help. Look how that turned out." Donnie frowned. "I was trying to help. You know how long it took me to find anyone that would hire me after the Burrs let me go?"

"But you found work here where they ranch a lot of the animals that are used in the rodeo." Jack looked around. "We inspected the bull that threw Lucas."

"Vets do that. I just tend to them."

"But you were there that night. You were part of the crew bringing them?" Jack asked.

"Sure. Work's work."

Jack looked Donnie in the eyes. "Did you do something to sabotage Lucas' ride? Something to the bull?"

"They'd have seen it if I had." Donnie shrugged it off.

"Something to the rope then?" Jack pressed.

"He got what he deserved. Thinking he's better than everyone," Donnie replied.

Jack shook his head. "He thought you guys were stealing. He cares about his staff. He cares about these animals. I've seen it. You wanted revenge but you weren't honest about your motives."

"Doesn't matter now. The boss here saw your pictures in the paper. He thinks I was cagey about why I was let go because Lucas hit on me. Now I'm a hero for not ratting someone out. I like it here—don't be a jerk," Donnie said.

"You could've gotten Lucas killed or anyone else in the ring helping. Or the bull. You don't care?" Jack asked.

"I didn't hurt the bull. I just gave him a bit of a bump. Like a steroid. I know how to do a proper injection so it didn't hurt the animal. He just had an extra spring in his step. Nothing your boy toy can't handle," Donnie admitted.

Jack balled his fists. "You could've gotten Lucas killed."

"He's fine. Maybe he learned a lesson. But you best put your fists down. This boss is real money. Cameras everywhere. Can't steal from him but he pays better. No nonsense." Donnie moved on to the next stall.

Jack pulled his cell phone from his pocket. "And I just recorded your confession. We'll see what your boss and the rodeo runners think about your working with their animals anymore."

"Shady ass." Donnie lunged at Jack.

Jack jumped to one side and tripped Donnie. "You don't want to fight me. Then it's an assault charge on top of all of it."

# Chapter Seventeen

Mama and Greg were in the stands and Lucas was staring at the bull he was about to ride. Staff members were trying to corral the bull into a shoot.

"Okay?" Tim asked.

Lucas nodded. "I wish Jack was here but I can't make him okay with this job."

"True. But you haven't given it a real chance with him either. You also haven't given an interview since that crap came out." Tim gave Lucas the side-eye.

"Jack asked me not to make it worse." Lucas held up his hand. There was no perfect answer this mess.

"I know but you gotta talk to the news some time. They'll swarm you after. All the Dallas papers are here. Legit ones are covering you tonight. Go give them the truth. Take the fall for it. Jack's innocent and wonderful. You should've waited until the medical stuff was over. You wish you could fix it and come out properly to the media before so you and Jack can be a couple." Tim shrugged.

"They'll spin in some other way," Lucas said.

"Not every place is the *Tattler*. You make it romantic and you're the good guy trying to win him back—they'll eat that crap up and you know it," Tim said.

"But he'll think I'm doing it for the publicity. It won't change his mind," Lucas insisted.

"That guy lost his job for you. He fell hard for you and wants you safe. You really think he won't know if you're being genuine?" Tim asked. "Even if it doesn't change his mind about the rodeo—it'll prove you love him. You want to protect him."

"Jack'll probably be moving away to avoid me," Lucas said.

"No, he's opening his own PT place. I ran into one of his cousins."

Lucas shot Tim a look.

"What? Small town. It'll be all over when you quit hogging the news with your comeback. Maybe an interview will help you get ready," Tim suggested.

Lucas looked over at his friend. "You think I'm not ready?"

"You're twitchy. You're not normally twitchy. Sometimes an injury changes you. It's okay," Tim said.

"I'll never be ready or the same," he said.

"Then be yourself now. Get it out there." Tim patted Lucas on the shoulder.

"Lucas Burr." Mr. Paxton walked up and eyed Burr.

"Paxton, to what do we owe the pleasure?" Lucas shook his hand.

Paxton sighed. "Your little gay friend paid my ranch a visit. He found out one of your fired hands ended up on my payroll. I didn't know he was fired for stealing or I'd never have approved it. Either way, Jack backed Donnie into a corner and got him on tape admitting he'd spiked your bull. Adrenaline or something he swiped from the vet."

"Donnie did it? Why the hell would he steal? I paid him fair, and he got more days off than most ranches." Lucas couldn't believe Jack had gone to the trouble after things had fallen apart.

"He wanted revenge. He thought you didn't listen to him about the stealing. I'll send you the audio file. Police have it. I fired his ass, of course. The stealing, well…if what he's saying is true about stealing to help the other hand who was undocumented…it's not right. You were right to fire them but seems like the guy wasn't alone. Trying to provide for a family of illegals in Texas with ICE all around…I wouldn't change a thing you did—but you should be more careful hiring. You could get in trouble for hiring people without docs. Not worth it." Paxton nodded.

Lucas shrugged. "Good ranch hands are hard to find. Thanks for the help. Hope the bull didn't suffer any real damage."

"Nah, but I don't think we should rodeo it again. Vet said that could affect the animal's heart. We don't need it having a damn heart attack in the ring. Hurting people and dying in front of kids. Might breed it or something. Not your fault though. We never meant you any harm." Paxton reach for Lucas' hand.

They shook on it. "Thanks."

Lucas stood there for a moment in shock. Donnie was a nice guy, and his theft had surprised most people. Now it made sense but Donnie had crossed lines from helping to trying to hurt people. And Jack had gone above and beyond on his own to track down Donnie.

Donnie had been right under their noses. Lucas needed to talk to Jack. It was all a lot clearer now.

Lucas had been wrestling with so much. Not talking with Jack was killing Lucas. What he wanted versus what others wanted him to do. Rodeo was in his blood but the urge to get back on the bull was coming from the outside.

His manly ego wanted to prove he was as good as he had been before the fall but he couldn't forget that pain. No other fall had hurt like that. Some would call him a coward but the young adrenaline junkie inside him wasn't all that mattered anymore.

He walked over to the press area and a million questions flew at him.

He held up his hand and they finally quieted down and the camera flashes stopped.

"I wanted to thank you all for coming out. I'm happy to be back to my old self. But I only have one person to thank for that and the papers haven't been very nice to him. Jack Gable is the best physical therapist in the state. He pushed me, didn't take crap or let me slack. I tried my best charm and I'm the one who fell for him and crossed the lines. He told me about the rules, the patient-caregiver thing, but I couldn't help myself."

"Are you saying that you forced him?" a woman shouted form the press group.

"No, no. That's not what I mean. We both…when it's right, it's right. True love can't always follow the rules. I'm sorry it cost him so much. People have been awful to Jack. He lost his job, and he deserves to have his privacy and life back. I hope you'll all leave him be."

"But you're gay?" another reported demanded.

"I am gay. I fought the feelings most of my life because of how my father viewed it. How the rodeo world treats gays isn't always kind. It was far worse when I was a kid and it scared me. I'm hoping to help change that being out and part of owner of Burrwood Rodeo," Lucas answered.

"Are you still together?" someone else asked.

"I love him but he's too smart to get stuck with a guy who falls off bulls for a living. My job is dangerous and he has warned me over and over that I could do real damage to myself every time I ride. Any of us out there, one fall and landing the wrong way and we're done. Dead or lucky to be in a wheelchair. Jack knows it and I know he's right." Lucas adjusted his hat.

"You're not riding?" someone asked.

"No, I'm a sucker for the ride. Just pray I don't land back in the hospital. Have a good night," he said.

Lucas turned and walked away as the group shouted more questions.

Tim nodded his approval.

"Jack's not coming back," Lucas said.

"Not with that attitude. If he loves you, he might give you another shot. If you live through it or meet him halfway," Tim said.

The bull was ready, stomping and shaking its head trying to find a place to go. Lucas waited for a moment of calm and slid onto the wild animal. The bull kicked and snorted. The feeling was familiar but not exactly the same…

The scraping of the metal gate, the buzzer, the lurch—Lucas' body remembered the cues and held tight. He'd never ridden this bull so he had to stay loose and try not to anticipate. It was the general rule but some bulls were predictable—they always threw a rider left or tried to launch him over their horns.

This bull was jumping, leaping and twisting his body, trying to shake Lucas off. Every landing was hard, jostling every bone in Lucas' body.

Fear gripped his heart and he couldn't even feel the rest of his body. Lucas tried to blot out the fear—that was a sure way to get hurt. But his body wasn't what it used to be. He was back in the saddle, so to speak, but he wasn't as strong. He was definitely not as fearless as he'd used to be.

He ignored the huge screen following him but when it cut to the stands, he spotted Jack with the paramedics and ambulance in a split second. He actually came? Was it his imagination? He relaxed his grip for a second and the bull bolted one way then turned.

The jerking and slamming reminded Lucas of his injuries but he held on. Getting thrown at the right time and trying to manage the fall was an art. He knew he should hang in there longer, let the people enjoy it a bit more. The crowd was roaring and that felt as good as ever.

But he saw an opening to bail with enough helpers positioned to grab the bull's attention. It was the safe move, the smart move. Lucas timed it right and let go—letting the bull do the work by tossing Lucas toward the wall.

Lucas hopped up, no harm done. He waved to the crowd but instead of exiting the ring, he headed right for Jack. It wasn't smart but it was what needed to be done. While he crossed the huge arena, he promised himself that that was his last rodeo ride. He'd work with new guys, promote the rodeo and show up for it as an owner but he was done risking his neck.

No matter what, he wasn't riding again. He had bigger plans for his life.

Jack tried to block out the jeering comments from the stands as he watched Lucas ride. People were blaming Jack for a lot of things. His heart pounded in his throat and his hands shook. Teddy stood by with a smile, confident as ever, but the paramedics had their eyes peeled for one wrong move.

"He'll be just fine. He's good," Teddy said.

"He'd probably be better if you hadn't ridden him too early and too hard. He would've been back weeks ago," joked another viewer.

"Lucas Burr is down but he's okay. Back up. Burr is back!!" the announcer shouted.

Jack couldn't even look. "That's it—he's fine. Let's go."

Jack stood up and pushed past Teddy and others while people in the stands made jokes about Jack joining Lucas under the bleachers.

Jack's face burned as he made it to the aisle when Lucas jumped over the wall.

"You came." He grabbed Jack.

Jack stepped back. "You shouldn't have done that. It's not good for your back. I can't believe you did so well. You're lucky." Jack tried to keep his composure. All the people around who'd been sneering and jeering were now quietly staring.

Lucas pulled Jack in. "You didn't hear my interview? You care too much and you hide it too well. I'm done hiding or fighting."

Jack shrugged. "I *tried* but I could barely sit through it. I love you but I can't live with it. I'm not asking you to quit but I can't put myself through it."

Lucas kissed Jack before he could figure out what else to say. The warmth and relief washed over him. Jack needed Lucas as much as he needed him.

"I swear, I'll do whatever you say with my back and the rest of my body. Just admit you love me in front of all these people," he said.

Jack caught a glimpse of them on the big screen. "The cameras are on us. We're up on that big thing for all to see."

"Don't care. I'm done. I'm out. I got back on the bull to prove I'm not a coward. I'm still me. I did it but I don't want that rush anymore. I had to try. I had to know it felt wrong. You're right, I want to ranch, I want you and a life. You're enough of an adventure and an adrenaline rush for me in bed. I don't mind training or helping with the rodeo but I'm not young enough to risk my neck anymore. I want a life." He leaned Jack down in a dip.

"Stop holding me like this. It's bad for your back," Jack scolded.

"Fine, I'll say it first. I love you and I'm not giving you up," he said.

Jack kissed him, pushing him to stand straight then sit down on the back of an open ambulance while Jack leaned over him.

"I love you too. But you have to promise me you're never getting on a bull again or an untamed horse," Jack demanded.

"I decided that the second I got on that bull. I tensed. I didn't want to miss my future with you for a few seconds of adrenaline. You seem to fire me up more than enough." He held Jack tight.

Jack wrapped his arms around Lucas' neck and kissed him. The crowd cheered but Jack heard nothing except that the man he loved had finally come to his senses.

# Chapter Eighteen

Three months later, *Back in the Saddle PT Group* opened with a full ribbon-cutting ceremony and cake. Lucas was there along with a bunch of his rodeo buddies. Jack had poached Teddy and tempted away a bunch of the best PT people from the hospital and home visits.

"It's perfect!" Josie declared.

There was a gym-like side for people nearing the end of their PT or who were ongoing and needed minimal supervision and a bunch of private rooms set up for newbies and people with more complicated issues.

"Do we get the tour?" Lucas asked.

Jack's aunt and uncle had turned up as well as Dot. They all followed along. "You see the two sides of work areas. Here in the middle we have the information center. People can get a fresh printout of the schedule, the orders and even make a doctor appointment if needed. Then we have the water, coffee and smoothie bar. Hydrating and keeping up energy is important."

"Are the smoothies any good?" asked a reporter.

"Try one," Lexi offered. "This winter we'll add hot teas but this green tea maccha smoothie can be customized with fresh fruits and various vitamin boosts. Perfect for a hot summer day in Texas."

Jack smiled. He'd even stolen the secretary and let her do something she loved more—mixing smoothies and healthy drinks. Dreams didn't have to be taking over the world or being a billionaire.

People tried the samples and enjoyed them. The video screens around the areas ran healthy videos about cooking, smoothies and stretching exercises, interspersed with sports, news or talk TV.

"Rumor is that your former employer was planning on launching a new office and expanding his PT business. Did you swipe the idea?" a reporter asked.

"Well, they let me go. That was my first ever misstep in my entire professional career—I was never written up or dismissed from anywhere before. I think they overreacted and I want a place to work that is professional but realizes that we're all human. Some people heal at a different rate. Some have different job, family or economic challenges that make physical therapy harder. Sometimes you have a therapist who isn't a good fit for a patient. Sometimes the fit is too good. The answer isn't to dismiss good workers or patients in need. The only way to have that sort of place is to own it," Jack explained.

He fielded a bunch more questions and seeing his parents there, proud of him, meant a lot. Lucas squeezed his hand and that meant everything.

* * * *

Finally, home after a celebratory dinner with both of their families, Lucas locked the door to the guest house.

"Am I being rude to my family?" Jack asked.

"What? Having them at the main house? Please, Mama loves entertaining. Everyone is exhausted. And we need privacy." Lucas started stripping off his clothing.

"I can't believe you moved me in here so fast." Jack slowly shed his clothing as well. "I keep waiting for Roscoe to dart in and start barking his head off."

Lucas smiled. "Mom and Baby love the new company. He's got more room to roam and people always around. Miss him in your bed more than me?"

Jack held up his hands in surrender. "Not a chance. The ranch expansion is working well. My mom is thrilled I scored a rich and influential cowboy."

Pulling a naked Jack down on the plaid couch, Lucas felt like he knew exactly where his life was going. "I'm starting a mentorship program with the rodeo guys. The big ranch house is a lot but I've been thinking we could turn it into a B&B and have a rodeo weekend package."

"We still live here?" Jack asked.

"Definitely." Lucas pinched Jack's ass and gave it a quick smack. "Mama could run the B&B. She loves the attention and entertaining in the big house. We have the privacy."

"I'm in." Jack moved to suck Lucas' cock.

Lucas shifted so he sprawled out on the couch, pulling Jack on top of him for a sixty-nine. "Good. Show me."

Lucas smacked Jack's ass as he fucked his boyfriend's face. Jack moaned and sucked, his hips trying to get more relief on his own dick. Lucas nipped and licked Jack's cock playfully. He sucked on his balls and spat on his asshole. The more Jack squirmed, the harder it was to keep from coming down his throat.

"You first." Lucas squeezed Jack's ass.

The moans of approval and need pushed Lucas closer to release. Since that night at the rodeo, they'd been screwing like they were wild animals in heat. But their trust built and knowing just how to get each other off was more fun, until they found a new way to make it better.

Lucas let Jack breathe. "You're holding out on me," Lucas scolded.

"You want me coming all over your ma's old couch?" Jack taunted.

Lucas spanked his ass again. "All over anywhere I want. Next you're going to want me to tie you down."

Jack moaned. "Don't tease."

Lucas slid his cock back into Jack's eager mouth. "You'll love the rough feel of the rope on your slapped ass. Around your cock so you can't come until I'm ready."

Jack bobbed his head on Lucas' erection, wanting his reward.

Lucas tongued around Jack's asshole. "Maybe you need a toy up your ass tonight, not my dick? If I'm not getting you off enough?"

Groaning, Jack grabbed Lucas' ass and fingered him while he fucked his face on that cock. Lucas gasped and lifted his hips for more of that extra effort. When Jack smacked Lucas' rear, he grinned.

"You think you can rope and ride me?" Lucas asked.

Jack slapped Lucas' ass with one hand and slid two fingers into him, fucking him, and sucking him all at once.

Lucas tried to keep control but he thrust into Jack's mouth. "Good, I can take was much as you can." He grabbed Jack's cock and held it back and licked the balls while jerking that hard cock on his chest and neck. Slapping that cock while rimming Jack, Lucas knew Jack'd blow in seconds.

Jack moaned and muffled his shouts on Lucas' body as he came.

"Fuck me," Jack said.

Lucas pushed Jack on the floor, missionary, like their first time, only Jack was on the receiving end. They'd both been tested so screw the condoms. "You want it dry?"

"There's lube in my wallet," Jack said.

Lucas grinned. "Of course." He found it and applied it. "You want to spank and rope me?"

Jack nodded. "Whatever gets you off."

Lucas slid into Jack's tight ass and felt a hand slap his rump. Jack wasn't wasting time playing it both ways.

"You got me close already. I don't think there's time to play," Lucas warned.

"Hard and fast and then we play?" Jack teased.

"If you'll cooperate." Lucas grabbed Jack's ass and thrust roughly into him.

"I love you," Jack said.

Lucas leaned down and kissed, biting him lips playfully. "I love you too. Now you show me how much."

Jack lifted and they rocked, groping and groaning for more. Lucas screwed Jack's brains out until they were both satisfied and noticed they'd tipped over the coffee table. The ring would have to wait.

"Ready for more?" Jack asked.

"Wait…next weekend, we need to go to Dallas." Lucas kept Jack pinned playfully.

"Okay. Why?"

"I made a tattoo appointment to get one to match yours," Lucas said.

"You don't have to." Jack tried to sit up.

"No, I don't. I want it." Lucas kissed him. "Just like I want to hear all your ideas for the ranch. We just always seem to end up fucking our brains out instead of finishing that conversation."

Jack blushed and grinned. "I want to tie you to the bed upstairs and spank you."

"I promise that will happen but first…your good ideas." Lucas sucked on Jack's nipples.

"Now? Really you think I can think of the public or business?" Jack squirmed.

"Get hard again. I don't care. I'll wait. I like watching you jerk off," Lucas warned.

Jack moaned. "Second-chance ranch section for animals that are discarded, abandoned or saved from a bad situation. Maybe also a therapy component?" Jack suggested.

"For the animals?" Lucas asked.

"I'm not really sure how that'd work. For people. Though maybe it'd sort of serve the same purpose for those animals. Once we know they're safe, of course. Horse therapy is used with a lot of people in rehab or with PTSD. Bunnies are used for people with a fear of horses. Grooming and working with animals is soothing. Might help some people along with that program. Talk to some veterans' organizations." Jack smiled.

"And you turn a charity effort into a new business," he teased.

"We don't have to charge much. Make it an outpatient part of other therapies," he replied.

"You got your dad's head for business," Lucas said.

"Dad. Mom. Your mom. We really don't need to talk about any of them now. Please can we table that conversation until the morning?" Jack groped Lucas' cock.

Lucas kissed Jack slowly, to torment him a bit more. "Okay. But I seriously doubt you'll be able to punish my ass before you fuck it."

"I'll just have to keep trying and practicing until I get it right." Jack kissed Lucas. "A cowboy's work is never done."

## Want to see more from this author? Here's a taster for you to enjoy!

# Hard Evidence: Under His Protection

## Cheryl Dragon

### *Excerpt*

"Cartel activity in Austin is up. Not just with street-level drugs, but known members have been seen. We are in contact with the DEA, but we're not sure what's going on yet. Violent crimes have been ticking up in the past week. Obviously, Narcotics has the lead, but we're just as involved. Work your cases, but also check on your local connections. Outreach helps," Lt. Ridgeway explained.

The Violent Crimes department briefings were normally duller, but Detective Matt Blackburn had only been in the unit a few months. Not that long ago, he'd been a patrol cop in uniform.

"Blackburn," Ridgeway said.

"Lieutenant," Matt replied.

"You're the most recent off patrol, so your connections are the freshest. A lot of this is happening on your old beat, so don't be afraid to go back to your old haunts and show off the suit." Ridgeway winked.

"Yes, ma'am." Matt nodded.

Some of the men bristled at working for a woman, but even Texas had to get with the times sooner or later…

Cartel trouble wasn't something that the area had issues with. Drugs, sure, but what city didn't have that problem?

"It's kind of far north for cartel activity," Matt said to his partner as the meeting broke up.

Julie shrugged. "You can't predict it. Maybe too much activity at the border… Maybe someone stole a shipment and ran north or someone escaped and made it this far. Cartels don't like to lose people, product or money. It might just be a few cartel guys and some hired staff looking to recover something."

"There's a shelter I used to keep an eye on. Mind if we roll by?" Matt asked.

"Sounds good to me. What kind of shelter?" she inquired.

"LGBTQ+ youth—some outreach programs but mainly a shelter. Teens can get themselves in trouble quicker than anyone." Matt refilled his travel mug with coffee then they headed to their vehicle.

"You got that right. Drive, since you know the area." She tossed him the keys. "Luckily the cartel probably won't mess with them. They'll be after their problem and gone. Drawing more attention only makes their lives harder."

"Sure, but some of those kids have been in gangs or sold drugs. Most have sold other things, but it's a complicated lot. I worked security for them sometimes when they had events," Matt shared.

"Any cute guys work at this shelter?" Julie teased.

"No. It's about the kids—and I'm not into kids," Matt said firmly.

"You need a life," Julie said.

He drove in the direction of the shelter. Austin traffic was crazy, as usual. "I got a promotion. That's a life."

She rolled her big blue eyes at him. "But you have no one to celebrate with. The Violent Crimes unit can be a rough place. You need something happy in your life to balance it out. Get a puppy, at least."

Matt chuckled. "Naturally, and when will I train and take out this puppy with a job so unpredictable, as well as being on call some nights?"

"Getting a boyfriend would help. Then get a couple of kids and make them do the grunt work. That takes care of things for me," Julie said.

Her hubby taught school, so he kept a regular schedule and the kids were at the same one, so childcare was managed. They were so cute, but life didn't fall into place for everyone like it had for Julie.

Matt found himself a bit jealous at times—not wanting Julie's husband, but she had a certainty about her life. She loved her work, but family came first.

"I'll try to get a life, just for you. But with a new job learning curve to manage, it might not be the best time." Matt had mastered deflecting set-ups and pushiness. He was a new detective, but plenty of other cops had tried to fix him up during his years on the force. *Next, she'll suggest the bars or gay apps.*

"You know, a cousin of mine has had a lot of luck on the apps," Julie said.

Matt smiled. "For hookups, sure. I'm not hurting in that area. I can walk into a gay bar and get a guy. It's fun, but it's not—"

"Love. Aww-w," Julie said.

"Real," Matt corrected her quickly. "It's not *real*."

"Real love. Have you thought about a little something? A rainbow pin on your lapel maybe? You are a hyper-suit masculine guy, which is you, but you're so... Half the department is still convinced you're straight," Julie said.

Matt shrugged and finally neared the block for the Engles Memorial Shelter. "Jules, not every gay guy is flamboyant. Not every lesbian is butch. I don't need to advertise."

"I know that. I didn't mean you should change yourself at all. I just don't know if you give off the right signals. You're all about the job at work," she said.

Parking the car, Matt looked at his partner. "Am I not paying enough attention to the people we deal with?"

"No, you're good with victims and suspects, even with community outreach. You talk plenty, but it's about the case or them and *their* lives," she said.

"They don't want to talk about me. We're public servants. I'm not picking up guys who commit violent crimes and I'm sure as hell not taking advantage of a victim," he said.

"You're right. And if another cop was interested in you, I'd have heard about it. So I need to find someone to set you up with," Julie threatened.

"Please don't. I'm fine. I have horrible timing and bad luck. That's all. I'm leaving it up to fate," Matt replied as he cut the engine.

"You're going to be the weird spinster uncle at my family holidays. I can see it now. Let's go, Mr. Fate," she teased.

The duo walked into the shelter and the kids turned to look.

"Blackburn got the day off?" one of the kids asked.

"Thanks for noticing, Mario. No, I'm a detective now," Matt said.

"Detective?" Minnie stuck her head out of the office. "We were wondering what happened to you." The petite woman with short, spiky purple hair wore a flowery print dress. Min ran out and gave him a hug that lifted her off her feet. "Congrats!"

"Thanks." Matt set her down. "This is Julie, my partner."

Minnie shook Julie's hand. "Hey. Happy to have the support. Want the tour—or do you have something specific to discuss?"

"Just increased trouble in the area. See any new dealers or problems?" Matt asked.

"Nothing new that I've seen, but I'll spread the word. We got our outside lights fixed, thanks to Josh, so that helps," she said.

"Is he around?" Matt tried to sound casual. The shelter was brightened by art, but the core of the building was gray and cold. Matt had done some maintenance and was glad others pitched in to keep the place safe and functioning.

"Who is Josh?" Julie asked with a raised eyebrow.

"One of our volunteers. He works at a rehab facility by day. As a certified addictions counselor, teens are his specialty, so he gives us part of his time. So sweet. Here he just uses AA methods and he even taught the kids to run meetings for when he can't be here, but it really helps. He's also kind of handy...and good-looking." Minnie smiled.

Matt had seen Josh around a lot when he'd patrolled the area. They'd exchanged glances that made Matt want more but had only traded small talk a few times when he'd helped out at the shelter. He'd thought there were sparks, but...

"You can't keep kids under eighteen. They go to the foster system, right?" Julie asked.

Minnie shared a look with Matt. "Of course... We house eighteen through the mid-twenties. We get a lot of minor teens who drop in for a meeting, a kind word or help with a parent issue, though. Josh and Matt were behind our family outreach."

"You worked with this Josh? Is he really cute?" Julie asked.

"They sort of worked in tandem. We're running on duct tape and good vibes, so we take help when and how we can get it. Josh is very attractive, but until fairly recently, he had a guy," Minnie explained.

"We never worked *together* on anything," Matt added.

"Sure you did—but not at the same time." Minnie waved a hand at him. "Josh suggested in one of their AA group-share things that, if they were underage and at risk of getting dumped into the system, they should reach out to other family members if they weren't safe at home. Maybe they could spend the summer there or even move—with parental permission, of course."

"Of course," Julie said and shot Matt a look.

PRIDE
PUBLISHING

# About the Author

A lover of unusual things, Cheryl Dragon enjoys writing unique stories with sinfully hot erotic romance. She loves cats, coffee and book signings where she can meet her fans. Cheryl lives in the Chicagoland area.

Cheryl loves to hear from readers. You can find her contact information, website details and author profile page at https://www.pride-publishing.com

www.ingramcontent.com/pod-product-compliance
Lightning Source LLC
LaVergne TN
LVHW091049080826
845145LV00002B/683